MW00893205

The Blue Marble

Susan R. Lawrence

God bless you!
Susan Lawrence

The Blue Marble

Copyright © 2016 Susan R. Lawrence

All rights reserved. This book or any portion thereof may not be reproduced or used in any manner whatsoever without the express written permission of the author except for the use of brief quotations in a book review.

www.susanrlawrence.com
srlauthor@mchsi.com

Dedicated to my seven favorite marble collectors: Bailey, Cadence,

Gabby, Michail, Grayer,

Benson, and Giana.

I love you to the moon and back.

Chapter One

Matthew! Matthew!"

I cringed when I heard mom's voice. After finishing my Cocoa Puffs, I'd slipped out to the backyard, hoping she didn't need me to watch my sister, Gabby.

The Saturday morning sunshine promised the kind of warm spring day when a ten-year-old boy wants to be outside and hang out with his friends. Not stuck in the house with a five-year-old while his mom works on her computer.

I shrugged as if I could shake my family off my back.

Then I snuck around the back of the garage, looking for Dusty, my best friend. I didn't see him in back, so I went on the worn strip of grass between our two yards to the front.

Dusty spotted me and waved. He carried his blue Tony Hawk skateboard with red flames. "I was just coming to get you. I'm headed over to the dollar store. Wanna come?"

The store stood in a strip mall across the street and through some empty lots. The huge parking lot provided great skate boarding. Lots of older kids hung around, doing cool moves.

I trudged onto his driveway. "Mom just called me. She wants me to watch Gabby so she can work on her computer."

"On *Saturday*? That's cruel."

"Yeah," I agreed. "But sometimes she has to work weekends." I didn't add that it was usually after she'd taken time during the week to take me to baseball practice or Gabby to dance lessons.

He cocked his head. "She's not calling now."

I made a face and sighed. "I have to ask permission to go across the street, and then she'd make me stay in the house."

"You could just go with me, and when we got back, you could say you were with me in the backyard, but we didn't hear her."

I frowned, considering Dusty's tempting idea. Finally I shook my head. "No, I don't think I should."

"Okay. Suit yourself. See you later." Dusty trotted down the driveway, glanced both directions, and darted across the road.

I slumped on the concrete driveway, my back against the garage, and watched until he disappeared behind the dentists' office. Everything was quiet at my house. Maybe Mom had convinced Gabby to watch TV or play a video game. Maybe she didn't need me to entertain her.

I stood up and walked to our garage. My skateboard hung on the wall between two hooks. It had come from Target and didn't have flames painted on it. Mom had said it was all we could afford. Ever since Dad hadn't come home from the war in Iraq, we didn't have much money. Mom said we needed to trust God to take care of us. I wasn't so sure. If God takes care of us, how come he didn't keep my dad safe?

Mom hadn't called a second time. I could hurry over, skate with Dusty for a few minutes, and then come back. Besides, Mom always gave me permission to go to the dollar store; she just wanted to know when I left the yard.

I lifted my skateboard from the hooks. Being careful not to bump the car, I stepped on the board, holding my hands up as I balanced. I pictured myself catching air, grinding, and doing ollies. Then I stepped off and tucked my skateboard under my arm. Walking out of the garage, I looked back at my house.

"Sometimes I wish I didn't even have a family." I'd whispered the words, but I felt them hang in the air as if I'd screamed them.

I checked for traffic and bounded across Canterbury Lane. In the empty lot, I skirted around a parked bulldozer. Another new house was being built. Yesterday a huge, round truck had poured wet cement into the hole that would be the basement of someone's house. Dusty and I'd watched the construction workers on our way home from school. Until my mom drove up and made me come with her and do chores.

I scuffed my feet through the dirt, kicking at random clods and watching them burst apart into little explosions of dust. Then, right between my green-and-white Nike shoes, something shiny caught my eye. I swung back to kick it out of the way. Changing my mind, I crouched in the dirt. Maybe it was something valuable, a buried treasure I could sell. Then I could buy a Tony Hawk skateboard. And help Mom out with the bills.

I dug down until I pried it loose. It was round and hard, the outside crusted with dirt. I rubbed some of the grime off with my thumb and held it up. The glass marble caught the rays of the morning sun. Strands of blue, the color of the spring sky, seemed to move and twirl inside. Totally worthless. I cocked my arm back to throw the marble into the yawning concrete hole.

Without knowing why, I stopped, rubbed it once more with my thumb and dropped it into the pocket of my jeans.

Suddenly a cloud of dust, much larger than the ones my feet had kicked up, caught me and spun me around. I squinted, then shut my eyes tightly against the swirling particles of dirt. A roar, unlike anything I'd ever heard before, filled the air. The cloud whirled faster and faster, and when it finally stopped, I dropped to the ground like a missed pop fly. The noise faded slowly, leaving my ears ringing. I shook my head to clear them. Cautiously, I opened one eye.

Both eyes flew open in amazement.

Chapter 2

I lay flat on my back in a field of sweet-smelling plants. Sitting up slowly, I rubbed the dirt out of my eyes. My house was gone. Dusty's house was gone. There were no houses in front or behind me. The bulldozer, the basement of the new home, the dollar store—all were gone.

I scrambled to my feet and turned in a circle. A farm sprawled in the distance beyond several hills, the big red barn like a painting against the blue sky. A white, two-story house stood beside it.

Maybe I'd been swept away by a tornado, like the one that carried Dorothy off in *The Wizard of Oz*.

"Help!" I meant to shout the words, but my voice came out in a squeak that sounded scary in the great, empty field. I looked around again, but there was only the farm and it looked a long ways away. I brushed off my jeans, pulled some tiny green leaves out of my hair, and started toward it.

Walking in the field wasn't easy. The ground was lumpy, and the plants caught at my ankles. Once I tripped and fell hard on my stomach. For a moment I couldn't breathe. When I finally sucked in air again, I cried out, "Mom!" But I knew she couldn't hear me.

After a long time of stumbling through the field, I came to a road. A fence stretched as far as I could see. Reaching out a finger, I touched the three wires strung between sturdy wood posts. Every four inches or so, there was a little bit of a sharp wire piece poking out, just waiting to grab my pants or arm. The spaces between the wires were large, though. I scrunched my body as small as I could and stepped over the bottom strand of wire. Then I moved the rest of my body between the wires. I felt a wire poke my back as I stood up, and I heard my shirt tear. Now my mom would not only be mad I'd left the yard, she would scold me for tearing my shirt. But I'd made it through the fence.

Traveling on the road was a little easier, although the dust made me sneeze and sometimes rocks made my feet skid out from under me. Slowly, the big red barn came closer. As I topped the last hill, I could see two other farms in the distance. Each of them had a barn, too, and a house. But I didn't spot a single familiar landmark.

A long driveway led to the closest house and barn, and I turned in and took a few steps. A fence similar to the one I'd crawled through ran beside it. Several tan and white cows lifted their heads and gazed at me, their mouths working over thick wads of grass. Standing beside the open barn door were two huge, black horses, who swished long tails over their backs.

The house, dwarfed by the barn, still looked twice the size of mine. A front porch curled clear around the house. In the back-yard, clothes flapped on a line stretched between two posts.

Now what? Should I just walk to the house and ask them how to get back to Taylor Springs? Maybe someone would call my mom, and I could ask her to pick me up. I took another three steps down the driveway.

Just then, from out of the barn sped a ball of fur with a high-pitched, ferocious bark. I looked for a tree to climb. Then I saw the tail wagging like my mom's feather duster. I dropped to one knee. "Hi, dog. I won't hurt you. I just want to find my way back home."

The dog sniffed my outstretched hand, licked it, then moved to my face, licking me and wagging its furry body. With my face buried in the black-and-white hair, I didn't notice the boy until he spoke.

"Rags'll lick you to death if you let her."

I looked up. "I like dogs."

The boy wore a plaid shirt and overalls, the kind my little cousin wore. I didn't know they made them that large. His feet were bare and he carried a wire basket full of eggs. He stuck out a grimy hand. "I'm James. But everybody calls me Jim."

I stood and shook his hand. "Hi, Jim. I'm Matthew."

Jim stared at me. "You're not from around here."

"Ummm, I live in Taylor Springs."

Jim's freckled nose wrinkled slightly. "You do? Don't think I've ever seen you. We go to church in Taylor Springs."

"Maybe I could call my mom and ask her to pick me up?"

"Sure thing. Come on in."

I followed Jim across the yard and up two wooden steps onto the wide porch. Rags watched us, her plume of a tail still waving. On a bench, three cats lay curled up, sleeping. One stretched, yawned, and rubbed against my leg. I gave her a pat before following Jim inside.

We walked into a large, sunny kitchen. Everything about the room looked strange and unfamiliar. A pretty brown-haired woman in a long dress stood by what must have been a stove, a huge and shiny white box on legs, with big black knobs in front. The woman stirred something in a black skillet. "How many eggs today?" she asked without turning.

"Ten." Jim set the basket on the floor. "Mom?"

She turned, and seeing me, her eyebrows rose. "And who do we have here?"

I stepped forward. "I'm Matthew Freeman. Somehow or other I got lost. Could you call my mom and ask if she'd come pick me up? I live in Taylor Springs."

"Why sure, honey." Jim's mom had a good mother voice: kind but not syrupy-sweet. I guessed she really liked kids, and didn't just pretend. "What's your dad's name?"

"My dad died in the war in Iraq. My mom's name is Lori. Her number is 832-5766."

A puzzled look came over her face. "That's too many numbers, Matthew."

"If you hand me the phone, I can call her."

Her frown deepened, and she wiped her hands on the ruffled apron tied around her waist. Then she walked to a strange looking wooden box hanging on the wall. A kind of horn protruded from the front. On one side was a handle, and on the other side hung another kind of device, attached

12

to the box with a cord. She held this one to her ear, turned the crank and spoke into the horn in front. "Shirley, this is Dorothy Hawthorne. I have a little boy here. His name is Matthew Freeman. He lives in Taylor Springs. Could you ring his house? His mom is Lori."

She listened for a bit, nodding and making little "ummm-hmmm" noises. I watched her face and her frown creases only deepened.

Finally, she hung up the little ear piece of the strange telephone. Then she sat in a chair. "Matthew, I'm sorry, but the operator doesn't have a listing for your mom."

Chapter 3

I wished I was my sister Gabby's age. She would be wailing and crying and carrying on. Ten was really too old to do that. So, I stood in the middle of that odd looking kitchen and bit my lip, swallowing back the tears.

"Maybe you could drive me back to Taylor Springs?" I choked out.

Jim's mom nodded. "Maybe. I don't drive. But Jim's dad will be in from the field at noon. Perhaps he could take you there after lunch."

Jim clapped his hands. "Swell! Can I take him up to my room, Mom?"

"Sure. And while you're up there, send Cathy down to set the table."

"Okay. Come on, Matthew!"

I followed Jim through a room with a huge round table and up some steep wooden stairs. At the top of the stairs, a long hallway sprouted rooms on either side.

At the first door, Jim stopped. "Mom wants you to go set the table."

A little girl, about Gabby's age, sat on a rug on the floor, reading a picture book. She looked up and saw me. "Who are you?"

"Friend of mine. His name is Matthew," Jim answered for me and continued down the hall.

Jim's room had a big bed covered with a quilt. A wooden chest sat on the floor beside it and there was a small shelf against the wall with toys

15

and books on it. Like the kitchen, everything looked so old fashioned. Maybe they were Amish.

Jim picked up a wooden model of an old airplane. "Me 'n' Dad built this. It's a Curtiss Warhawk P-40."

I reached out and touched one wing. "A Curtiss what?"

"Warhawk. The neatest fighting plane ever. My dad flew one in the war. He just came home a few months ago."

"Your dad flew a plane like this?"

"Sure did. He knows all about modern planes."

I scratched my head, trying to sort everything out. "My dad fought in the war, too."

"Was he in Germany?"

"No, Iraq."

Jim looked as puzzled as I felt. He pulled a cloth bag off the shelf. "Hey, ya wanna play marbles? I jus' bought a new shooter from Grayer's General Store."

I started to say I'd never played marbles. I'd only heard about playing from my grandpa. Then I remembered. My hand dipped into my pocket and pulled out the blue marble. "I found this on the way here this morning."

Jim squinted at the marble lying in my hand. "Somebody lost a good shooter. Oh, well. Finders keepers, huh?"

Just then his mom's voice drifted up through holes in the square iron grate on the floor. "Boys! Wash your hands and come for dinner."

16

My stomach rumbled. It had been a long time since my bowl of Cocoa Puffs this morning. It had also been a long time since I'd been to the restroom. Jim's mom had said to wash up. That must mean we would go to the bathroom, and I wouldn't have to ask where it was.

But no, we went to the kitchen and washed our hands in a round metal pan using a little bar of soap. Then we dried using the towel hanging on the side of the cupboard. I whispered to Jim, "Where's your restroom? I gotta go."

"Out there."

I looked where he pointed and couldn't believe it. He pointed outside, in the backyard, to a little wooden shack.

"That's where you pee?"

Jim nodded. "'Cept in the middle of the night. We can use the chamber pot, then."

I hurried out to the shed. Inside was a wooden bench with two oblong holes. I held my breath against the smell. I thought people used places like these only at big events like the Fall Festival in Taylor Springs. They brought in porta potties for every corner. And Gabby always whined if she had to use one.

When I got back to the house, everyone already sat at the dining room table. I hurriedly rinsed off my hands, dried them, and slid into the chair beside Jim.

A man who must have been Jim's father sat on the other side of Cathy. He was tall and muscular with a tan face and arms. He wore overalls like Jim's, only even bigger and dirtier.

17

He bowed his head and said, "Heavenly Father, thank you for this food that you have provided. Bless the hands that prepared it. Amen." Then he started passing the food around. I was almost glad I hadn't found Mom yet. There was fried chicken, the crispy kind that's juicy inside; mashed potatoes, smooth and creamy; coleslaw like my grandma makes; warm, buttery biscuits; and big glasses of milk to wash it all down. I heaped my plate full and went to work on it, not even listening to the flow of talk around me.

"Young man."

I looked up from my chicken leg to see Jim's father watching me. My mouth was full of food, so I just nodded to show I was listening.

"I understand you live in Taylor Springs."

I nodded again and swallowed the wad of chicken. "I live on Canterbury Lane."

"So what are you doing way out here?"

How did I answer that one? "I, uh, walked through a field."

Jim's dad kind of raised one eyebrow and looked at Mrs. Hawthorne—the kind of look adults give each other when they think there's more to the story. "As soon as lunch is over, I'll drive you home. I need to go to the feed store anyway."

"Thanks," I said, returning to my plate. As I scraped up the last of the crumbs, here came Mrs. Hawthorne with a chocolate cake, and each of us got a thick slice on our plates. I dug in without a word.

After lunch, Jim handed me a towel. "Would you like to help with the dishes?"

I nodded. "Sure." He handed me the dishes he'd washed and rinsed, and I wiped them clumsily with the towel. I wondered why they didn't buy a dishwasher.

Jim finished washing the last pan. He pointed to a metal bar on the side of the cabinet. "Jus' hang the towel over there."

As I draped it over the bar, I glanced up to see a calendar with a picture of an antique tractor. April 1946. I gulped. 1946!

"Jim?" He was handing dishes to his mom to stack in the cupboards. "Is your calendar for this year?"

"It'd be kind of silly to have last year's calendar, wouldn't it? Doesn't it say 1946?" He handed the last of the dishes to his mom and turned to me. "Let's go see if Dad's ready to go."

I couldn't move. I just stood there, staring at that 1946 calendar and trying to figure out what had happened.

"Matthew! Let's go." Jim waited, holding the screen door open for me and nudging a cat out of the way with his foot.

I jerked away from the calendar and followed Jim outside, the screen door banging behind us. Mr. Hawthorne pulled up in the shiniest antique truck I'd ever seen.

What had I done? How would I ever get home?

Chapter 4

The truck chugged down the road at about the speed of Gabby's battery-operated Barbie car. Mr. and Mrs. Hawthorne rode in the front seat with Cathy between them. Jim and I sat in the back of the truck, watching the farm grow smaller beyond the clouds of dust rolling behind the tires.

It seemed like we rode for a long time before we could see houses and buildings. I got up on my knees to watch over the side of the truck bed. Mr. Hawthorne slowed almost to a stop and leaned out the open window. "Can you tell me where to go, boy?"

I studied our surroundings. None of the buildings or houses or roads looked familiar. "I live on Canterbury Lane. It crosses Highway Seventy-three."

"Well, this *is* Highway Seventy-three. I'll go slow, and you holler when you see your street."

I sat and watched the old fashioned cars and the unfamiliar buildings and houses. At last I saw something I recognized: the large, stone library where Mom brought Gabby and me to check out books in the summer. I leaned forward and shouted, "I see the library!"

The truck slowed to a stop. Mr. Hawthorne's head hung out the window again, this time with a definite scowl. "Doggone it, boy. We're looking for your house. Not the library."

"I think we went too far. We're almost downtown."

Mr. Hawthorne backed the truck into the driveway of a restaurant advertising "Good Home Cooking." Then he turned back the direction we had come.

Jim kept asking, "Is it there? Is that it?" I shook my head again and again, each time feeling more frustrated and miserable.

When we reached the outskirts of town again, Mr. Hawthorne slowed and leaned out. "Still didn't see your street?"

"It's just not there." I shook my head.

The truck rolled to a stop. I could see Mr. and Mrs. Hawthorne talking in the front seat. She gestured with her hands, but he kept shaking his head. Then he turned to me again. "Are you positive your street crosses Highway Seventy-three?"

"Yes. At least it used to."

The truck backed up again and made another turn, back toward town. It sped up, and in a few minutes we were near downtown. We stopped in front of a dark brick building with broad steps that led to double wooden doors. The sign out front read Taylor Springs Children's Home.

I thought I knew what the building was, but I didn't want to find out for sure. I slid down in the bed of the truck. The truck doors clicked open and I heard footsteps as someone climbed out.

"Come on, Matthew," Mrs. Hawthorne called. "There are people here who will help you find your mom."

"Can I come in, too?" Jim scrambled over the side of the truck.

"That might be good." Mrs. Hawthorne reached out and tousled his hair before she put her arm around his shoulders. They waited as I stepped down over the tailgate, and then Mrs. Hawthorne led the way up the steps.

With each step, my feet grew heavier and the lump in my throat grew bigger. I had seen movies about orphans, kids whose moms and dads had died. My mom wasn't dead, and she was probably waiting for me in 2016.

Mrs. Hawthorne lifted and dropped a handle that made a loud knocking noise. A tall, thin lady opened the door so quickly I thought she must have been waiting just inside. She wore a long, black dress and her hair was pulled back into a bun. Tiny, wire-rimmed glasses dangled on a silver chain around her neck.

"May I help you?" In spite of her drab dress, her voice was pleasant and her smile kind.

Jim's mom spoke. "We live out in the country. This boy appeared on our farm this morning. He says he lives in Taylor Springs, but we've been driving around for an hour, and we can't find either his house or the street he says it's on. I thought maybe someone here could help locate his family."

The lady in black opened the door wider. "My name's Miss Bailey. I'm the director of the Children's Home. Come on in."

Jim's mom shook Miss Bailey's hand. "I'm Shirley Hawthorne."

Then, looking at me, the tall lady asked, "And what's your name?"

My mouth felt dry, and I swallowed hard before answering. "Matthew Freeman," I mumbled. I longed to run far away from this brick building with waxy-smelling floors.

"Let's go to my office." Her sturdy shoes tapped down the hallway to a small room. Piles of papers covered the wooden desk. In the middle of the clutter, sat a large, black machine with raised, round keys. Each key had a letter printed on top. Was it a typewriter?

"Please, sit down." She pulled open a drawer, rifled through the file folder, pulled out a form, and inserted it into the typewriter. "Matthew Freeman…F..r..e..e..m..a..n?"

I nodded. I didn't want to speak, because I was afraid that if I did, the tears gathering in my eyes would spill over.

"Is that correct?" Miss Bailey peered at me over the top of her glasses.

I raised my eyes to meet hers. "Yes." I nodded again.

"Your parents' names?"

"My dad was killed in Iraq. His name was Richard. My mom's name is Lori Freeman."

Her fingers poised over the keys, and as I gave her information, they sprang into action like five-legged bugs pouncing on their prey. I answered all of her questions and told her everything I thought would help, except the fact that when I woke up this morning it was 2016 and now it was 1946.

"Matthew, would you wait in the hall for a few minutes while I talk to Mrs. Hawthorne?"

I stood up and trudged out to the hall. A wooden bench sat against the wall, but I slid to the floor and sat cross-legged.

Jim followed me out and sat down beside me. "They'll find your mom."

I wasn't so sure. I strained to catch the conversation inside the office, but Mrs. Hawthorne had closed the door, and I could only hear bits and pieces: "Runaway...no phone listed...doesn't make sense..."

Miss Bailey murmured in response, and then Mrs. Hawthorne spoke again. "Sorry...can't help...just barely making it...husband...home from war..."

Then the door opened and Mrs. Hawthorne came out. "Come on, Jimmy."

Both of us stood up and Mrs. Hawthorne patted my back. "I just know they'll help you, Matthew." She gave me a sad little smile.

"Were not just leavin' him here are we?" Jim looked at me over his shoulder as his mother took his hand and tugged at him.

I wanted to race after him, but Miss Bailey stood behind me, her hand gripping my shoulder.

Chapter 5

The swish of Miss Bailey's long, black skirt made me think of Halloween stories of witches and evil. I tried hard to remember her kind expression when she opened the front doors.

Her voice sounded crisp and no nonsense, kind of like a teacher on the first day of school, when she wants you to be sure to follow all the rules. "I'm going to take you to the boys' dormitory. The others are still in school but will be here soon. I'll make a few phone calls this afternoon, see if I can find out anything more about your mom. Are you sure you've told me everything?"

"Uh-huh." I trotted to keep up with her as she strode down the hall. Through the glass in the front door, I could see Mrs. Hawthorne stepping into the truck. Jim climbed in the back. I swallowed hard, then took a deep breath and followed Miss Bailey up two flights of wide stairs.

She led me to a large room with tall windows lining one side. Against each wall was a row of beds. Most of them had a blanket pulled up neatly over a pillow.

"This will be yours." She patted a bed with a bare mattress. "I'll let Delilah know that you need a set of bedding. There's a shelf in the activity room with some books and games." She pointed across the room, where two doors stood slightly open. "Just find something to occupy yourself."

Her footsteps tapped back down the stairs. I walked down the row of beds. One door led to a bathroom, which I used, and I was relieved to see that the toilet flushed. Another door led to a large, open room. At one end was a big wooden box with what looked like a speaker on the front. It had some knobs on it, but I thought maybe I shouldn't try to turn them. A shelf held an assortment of books. Most of them looked pretty boring, but the title of one was *Daniel Boone.* I leafed through it and put it back on the shelf. There was a tall can of some building things called tinker toys, a set of farm animals, and two board games: Uncle Wiggily and Parcheesi. A round coffee can held an assortment of glass marbles. I picked up the book again and lay down on the floor. I tried to read, but all I could think about was home. How was I going to get back there?

I hadn't even finished the first chapter when I heard the rumble of many footsteps on the stairs. The door burst open, and about ten boys marched in.

The leader, a boy who topped my height by at least six inches, stopped abruptly when he saw me. The rest of the boys formed a circle around me. "You a new kid?"

"Ummm. I'm just here waiting while Miss Bailey finds my mom. I kinda got lost."

He made a snorting noise. "Huh. That's what they all say. I'm Ralph. I'm fourteen, and I'm in charge here."

Two sandy-blond haired boys stood side by side. The taller one spoke up. "You're not in charge, Ralph. You just wish you were." To me he said, "I'm John, and this here's my little brother, Lee."

"My name's Matthew." I gave them a polite smile.

One by one they told me their names: Pete, Frank, Donovan, Benny, and Bobby.

"How come you're wearing sissy clothes?" Ralph gawked at my shirt and jeans.

I scowled up at him. "I don't think they're sissy clothes. Mom bought them at Target."

"Target? Where's that?" Frank's eyes were wide.

I shook my head. "Just a store." Didn't they even have a Target in 1946?

The boys lost interest in staring at me and wandered off to play a game or read, except for one, who looked to be about my age, who sat down by me. Like all the other boys, he was dressed in dark-colored corduroy pants and a print shirt, but what I noticed most were his bright, carrot-red hair and the blast of freckles covering his face.

He pointed to my new Nikes. "I like your shoes. They're different."

"Thanks. You're Bobby, aren't you?"

He nodded. "That's me. People always know me by my hair. I think my mom had red hair. But I can't really remember." His face grew a little sad. "I like to think she did, anyway. I turned ten last week. I kinda hoped I would get a family for my birthday, but that didn't happen. Those of us on this floor are almost too old to be adopted. So...how come you're here?"

What could I say? That I had a family in 2016 and somehow I'd gotten stuck in 1946? "I don't remember everything. I just kind of woke up in a field, and I walked to the closest farm and the mom and dad drove me here and left me."

Bobby's eyes widened. "You mean you got amnesia? You don't know who you are?"

Great idea! "That's it. I know my name's Matthew, but I can't remember much else."

"I bet you got hit on the head. Maybe the Mafia did it! And your parents are searching everywhere for you. And then they'll give up someday and believe you are dead, and they'll have a funeral for you and everything."

Bobby jumped up and down with excitement.

I couldn't muster up any of the enthusiasm that Bobby seemed bursting with. "In the meantime, I'm stuck here."

"We can be detectives and search for your hidden past." Bobby leaned low. "I think we should just keep this secret, just between us." He glanced across the room, where Ralph was talking with a few of the older boys. "Not all the guys in here would be helpful, if you know what I mean."

At that moment a bell rang from somewhere downstairs. The boys scrambled to put away the games, toys, and books. They formed a line at the door. I put *Daniel Boone* back on the shelf, followed Bobby and stood behind him.

A short, thin man wearing a bright green bow tie appeared at the door. Thick glasses perched on a big, round nose, and large ears protruded on either side of his head.

The man looked at me without smiling. Then, with a quick nod of his head, he spoke. "I'm Mr. Garrett. You must be Matthew."

"Yes, sir." His grim face suggested I'd better use my best manners.

"You follow the rules and we'll get along just fine."

"Yes, sir."

Mr. Garrett turned on his heel and we marched behind him, out the door and down the hall.

"Where are we going?" I whispered to Bobby in line ahead of me.

The line stopped abruptly. "No talking!" Mr. Garrett turned and glared over the line behind him. Then we resumed the march.

Bobby looked over his shoulder and made eating motions with his hands and mouth.

When we got to the dining room I was amazed to see girls—all ages and sizes. They wore flowered dresses in similar styles and seemed to be in charge of setting food out and serving it. Our line of boys filed past a window, where we picked up a heavy plastic tray and a metal fork. Then we were given a plate of food, a carton of milk, and an apple. I looked at the noodle mixture spooned over mashed potatoes and thought longingly of cheeseburgers and fries from McDonald's.

The other kids ate without talking, forking heaping mouthfuls down as if they might not get another meal. I pushed the food around my plate and finally drank my milk and bit into my apple.

"Are you going to eat that?" The skinny boy sitting next to me pointed his fork at my noodles.

"No. You can have it." I shoved the tray closer to him.

He glanced around furtively before diving in. "Thanks," he mumbled around a huge mouthful of the potatoes.

After supper, we all followed Mr. Garrett outside to a fenced area behind the main building. I could see two swings, a single metal slide, a set of three horizontal bars of varying heights, and a contraption you could sit on and spin around like a merry-go-round. The equipment was grouped around a huge oak tree with thick branches that shaded most of the playground.

Wishing I had a video game to play, I wandered around the perimeter, dragging my hand along the edge of the fence. In one corner, Bobby huddled with some of the other boys. I made the turn and followed the fence until I came to the group.

Bobby grinned up at me. "Hey. Want to play marbles?"

"I'll just watch." The game didn't look too difficult; you aimed a bigger marble at a bunch of smaller marbles until you knocked them out of the circle. I reached into my pocket and felt the smooth chill of the blue marble.

After a couple of games, I was almost ready to ask if I could join in when the doors swung open and the girls spilled over the playground. They gathered in small, giggling groups or stood in line, chanting rhymes, as they waited for the jump rope. A few of them took turns on the swings, pushing each other. One older girl held onto her skirt and ran across the playground to where we were circled around the marbles.

She tossed two long brown braids over her shoulders. "Are we playing keepsies?"

Ralph scooped up marbles from the circle drawn in the dirt before looking up at her. "No. Too many little kids cry if they lose."

"Okay." When she smiled, her brown eyes sparkled, and a small dimple appeared on one cheek. She reminded me of Gabby, even though she was older. I couldn't believe I missed my little sister. She took a clear glass marble out of a dress pocket. "I'm in the next game. Are you playing?" She looked at me.

"I haven't played much. And I don't have any marbles, except this one." I pulled the blue marble out of my pocket and held it out.

"Nice shooter. We can loan you some marbles. I'm Betsy." She held out her hand.

"Matthew." I shook her hand, thinking I'd never shaken hands with a girl before.

"Want me to teach you to be a sharpshooter?"

"Sure." I nodded, not sure at all. Did I want to learn from a girl?

"You two gonna play or chit-chat?" Ralph redrew the large circle in the dirt. The boys stepped behind one of the lines drawn on either side of the circle.

"I'm playing. Matthew's watching." Betsy joined the boys on the line. One by one they tossed their shooters toward the opposite line. Pete's marble landed closest to the line, Betsy's was next closest. Ralph arranged thirteen marbles in a cross formation at the center of the circle.

Pete knelt down at the edge of the circle and flicked his shooter at the cross. The marbles clicked and rolled, and one green marble went out of the circle. Pete put it in his pocket and stretched out for a second shot from

33

where his shooter lay. Flick! A yellow marble rolled out, his next shot took out a blue one, then a two-toned green one. On his next shot, he hit a white marble, but his shooter rolled out of the ring. Pete's turn was over.

Betsy knelt down, pushing her skirts out of the way, her forehead wrinkled as she concentrated. Her first shot netted her a white marble and her next two shots brought two more, but on her fourth shot she failed to knock any marbles out. She frowned and came to stand beside me. "I didn't focus on the distance to the circle."

Donovan shot next. Betsy stayed beside me, filling me in on every play. "Donovan's trying for that green one. If his shooter goes out, his turn is over. He could try for mine, too. Then I'd have to work from outside the circle. They do that sometimes, because I'm a good player." She didn't seem to be bragging, just stating facts.

Donovan pocketed only one marble.

Bobby was up. He knelt in the dirt and knuckled down. Three marbles ended up in his pocket. Pete was kneeling for his second turn when a loud buzzer sounded. There was a scramble as everyone grabbed for his or her marbles, stuffing them in their pockets or small bags and racing to line up. Two lines formed: one of boys, the other of girls. As I hurried by, I waved at Betsy. "Thanks for teaching me."

"It was my pleasure, Matthew. You give me one more boy to beat."

Mr. Garrett stood at the front of the boys' line. I took my place, being careful not to talk this time. When we arrived back in the bedroom, Mr. Garrett shoved a pile of clothes at me. "Here are your pajamas, Matthew, and a washcloth, towel, and toothbrush."

34

Bobby showed me the line of sinks, where I stood and waited for my turn. As I used the rough cloth to scrub my face, I thought of all the times I'd given Mom a hard time when she asked me to take a shower or brush my teeth.

My pajamas were itchy and too big, and they had little old airplanes all over them. Bobby's were made out of the same material. When we were ready for bed, we were allowed to go in the other room and listen to the radio, the big box I had seen earlier. It told a story about two men, Amos and Andy, who got into all kinds of trouble. They were pretty funny, but it was hard for me to sit and listen to something without watching it on a TV screen.

While everyone was listening to the show, Mr. Garrett stepped out the door and moved down the hall. Bobby leaned over to me, "He's got a bottle in his bedroom."

"A bottle?"

"Mr. Garrett drinks whiskey. We can smell it on him when he comes close."

"Is he allowed to do that?" I kept an eye on the door, certain he would return any minute.

Bobby shrugged. "I don't think Miss Bailey knows about it."

The show ended with lots of laughter and some applause laced with static. Without anyone directing us, we all trooped back into the bedroom. I climbed up on my bed and pulled the blanket up. The room felt a little chilly. I thought about my warm bed with the soft, thick blankets.

Bobby dropped to his knees beside the bed next to mine. "Don't you say your prayers?"

"Ummm. Yeah. I mean, I pray." I'd never actually gotten out of bed to pray, though. And I sure didn't plan on doing it tonight. Would I tell God I wanted to go back home? Would He even listen?

After a few minutes, Mr. Garrett shouted from the doorway, "Everyone in bed. Lights out." Then he flipped a switch, and the room was dark. I heard the springs on Bobby's bed squeak as he climbed into it.

I felt even further from home than I did last summer at Boy Scout camp. I missed Mom and Gabby. I swallowed hard to keep the tears away and turned my face into the pillow.

Maybe if I closed my eyes and went to sleep, I would wake up in my own bed, and this whole thing would be a dream.

Chapter 6

Boys up! All boys up!" Mr. Garrett's harsh shouts and the sudden glare of the overhead light jerked me from my slumber. So much for my thinking this was all a dream. All around me were the thumps of bare feet hitting the floor. I sat up and stretched. Some of the boys raced and pushed to be the first in the bathroom. Bobby carefully straightened his sheet and pulled the blanket up, smoothing out the wrinkles and tucking in the ends.

"When's breakfast?" I looked at the squares of dark sky outside the window.

"We have kitchen duty this morning. Mr. Garrett will be in here in just a few minutes." Bobby stripped out of his pajamas, folded them carefully and slipped them under his pillow. Then, from a basket under his bed, he pulled out clean clothes and dressed. "You'll be in trouble if you don't hurry up."

Kitchen duty? That sure didn't sound like the way I wanted to begin the day. I had no basket under my bed, so I pulled on my clothes I'd worn yesterday—my wonderful 2016 clothes. Even the torn shirt felt comfortably familiar.

"Come on, I'll help you." Bobby stood on the other side of my bed, tugging at the blanket.

"We have to make our beds?" I pulled at the blanket on my side. "What's the big deal?"

"Mr. Garrett straps boys who forget."

I was about to ask what he meant when Mr. Garrett walked in. He swung a leather strap and moved slowly down the center of the room, between the two rows of beds, slapping the strap on the palm of his hand so it made a loud pop. I tried not to jump every time it happened.

When he got to John and Lee's beds, he stopped. His nose wrinkled and he waved his arm toward the bed. "Peel back the blankets," he demanded.

Little Lee backed up against his brother. Then, with a fearful look at Mr. Garrett, he slowly pulled the blanket back.

"Why, lookie here, boys. Some *baby* wet this bed. One of the first-floor kids must have come upstairs." The leather strap hit his palm again. Thwack! "Bend over, boy."

Suddenly, John stepped around Lee, pushing him behind. "That's *my* bed, Mr. Garrett. I wet the bed last night."

Mr. Garrett glared at both boys. "Don't lie to me."

"I'm not lying, Mr. Garrett. I did it." John bent over, bracing himself by grabbing his ankles. Lee's eyes began to fill with tears.

The leather strap whistled through the air and struck John with enough force I was sure he would be knocked over. Thwack! He merely grunted and braced himself for the second smack. Thwack! I bit my lip to hold back the tears John refused to shed.

Mr. Garrett's mouth stretched into an odd little smile. "Strip that bed and get into line. We'll be late for kitchen duty." And he strode off to take his place in front. Bobby and I followed the rest of the boys. We didn't speak. We didn't even look at each other.

We marched after Mr. Garrett down a back stairway, our feet banging on the metal stairs. Like silent soldiers, we swished through some swinging doors leading directly to the kitchen.

A large, brown-skinned woman turned from the enormous pot she had been stirring. Her hair was wrapped in a cheerful red bandana, and a food-spotted apron covered all of her ample front. "Here's my help. I was beginning to think I was going to have to go upstairs myself and drag you all out of bed." There wasn't a hint of scolding in her voice and her smile was broad and kind. Mr. Garrett disappeared behind the swinging doors and I sighed with relief.

"Bobby, you come over here and keep stirring this oatmeal. Pete, you and Ralph get the bowls and spoons out. Frank, do you think you can help me make some toast? Johnny, you and Lee can put the milk out." As she gave the orders, each of the boys quickly moved to do as she asked.

Finally she looked at me. "And who do we have here?"

"I'm Matthew. I'm new here. But I don't think I'll be here long. Miss Bailey is finding my family."

She reached out one plump hand to ruffle my hair. "I hope she finds them. But for now, welcome to the kitchen of Children's Home. Some of us think it's the best room of all." She chuckled. "How about you help everyone, see where things are, so next time you come down you're ready

39

to help. My name's Jemma Jean. You just come see me if you have any questions."

"Okay. I can do that." I moved out into the dining room, where John and Lee were. I helped them bring the little bottles of milk from the cooler to the tables. As we finished the job, I turned to John. "You okay?"

"Yeah. It happens a couple times a week. I'm used to it."

"But … you didn't do it. You were in the bed next to Bobby's."

John gazed at me for a minute like he was trying to weigh the risks of trusting me. "You're right. Don't tell Mr. Garrett, though, okay? Lee can't help it. It's not like he tries to wet the bed. He just has nightmares."

I shook my head. "I won't tell."

Then we could hear the thunder of many footsteps. Minutes later, a whole herd of younger kids—some were just barely walking, some were babies carried by older girls—trooped into the dining room. I spotted Betsy carrying a little curly-headed girl, whose thumb remained planted in her mouth as they bounced along.

John grabbed my arm and pulled me into the kitchen, where we handed out slices of toast. Jemma Jean scooped spoonfuls of steaming oatmeal into each bowl, greeting every child by name.

After everyone else had received their breakfast, she filled bowls for us. It seemed to me that ours were fuller than those we'd handed out. Each of us got one thick slice of toasted bread, too. We carried our trays carefully and slid onto the benches, scooting and sliding our bowls until everyone was seated.

My stomach rumbled, and I didn't offer to share with anyone. After

40

eating, we all helped Jemma Jean do the dishes, scrubbing them in a huge sink of water and drying them with white towels. I thought longingly of the dishwasher at home. All we had to do was put the dishes inside. Couldn't we at least use Styrofoam bowls and throw them away?

As we hung up the towels on a long metal bar, Mr. Garrett appeared, and the line formed again. Bobby stood several boys ahead of me, so I couldn't even pantomime the question, where are we heading now?

I followed the line up the metal steps, past the bedroom, and up more steps to a third-floor classroom. Wooden desks stood in rows. A dusty black chalkboard stretched across one wall and posters on the other walls reminded us, "Always Do Your Best," "i before e, except after c," and "Friends Help Each Other." Girls already occupied some of the desks. Betsy sat by the window, her back straight and her eyes facing the front. A woman I guessed was the teacher wrote on the chalkboard with a stubby piece of white chalk. She turned to face us with a pleasant smile.

The rest of the boys slid into chairs, pulling books, paper, and pencils out of the opening in the front of each desk. I stood, waiting to be told what to do.

"Let me know if any of them cause you problems." Mr. Garrett left, and we could hear his feet clattering on the metal steps.

The teacher stepped toward me and asked, "Are you Matthew Freeman?"

When I nodded, she beckoned me forward. "Welcome to our class. I'm Miss Jones." She handed me a faded red book, a stack of lined paper,

41

and one yellow pencil. "This will get you started, and I'll get the rest of your books later. Where did you go to school last?"

I decided to stick to the story I'd told Bobby. "I had some kind of accident. I don't remember much. But I think I'm in fourth grade."

"Accident?" She looked at me and cocked her head. "Well, I'm glad you remember you were in fourth grade. That gives us somewhere to start. You may take the empty desk next to Frank." She stepped back and faced the whole group as I ducked into the seat she'd indicated. Frank turned to give me a quick smile.

"Good morning class. Please pass your math work to the front." She looked at a tall girl with a big nose and long, stringy hair. "Sharon is our helper this week. Would you collect the papers and put them on my desk?" The girl stood, smiled slightly, and gathered the papers from each row.

"Take out your spelling books please." Miss Jones flipped through the pages of a larger book like the one on my desk.

As the morning passed, I struggled to focus on classwork. My thoughts kept wandering to my family and whether I would ever get back to them. When a bell rang and Miss Jones announced, "Line up for recess," I sighed with relief.

Betsy stood in front of me, her braids tied with bright-blue bows that matched her dress. "Playing marbles today?"

My hand felt for the familiar lump of the blue marble. "Uh, yeah." I hoped I could remember all she'd taught me yesterday.

Miss Jones tied a scarf around her blond curls before leading us down the three flights of stairs and outside. The sky was the same shade of bright blue as Betsy's hair ribbons, and the sun spread warm fingers over the playground. I made my way to the group under the oak tree. Ralph had already drawn a circle flanked by two lag lines in the soft dirt.

I reached into my pocket to touch the blue marble. "Okay if I join the game?"

"Sure." Betsy and the boys were tossing their marbles from the lag line to determine the order of players. Frank stepped over and motioned for me to stand beside him and throw. Betsy's marble was the closest. She would go first, then Pete, then Frank. I would shoot fourth, and Donovan would be last.

On her turn, Betsy pocketed four marbles, Pete collected three, and Frank got one.

It was my turn. I knelt at the edge of the circle and placed my blue shooter on the edge. My hand went knuckles down next to it. I tucked in my thumb and popped it out. Flick! The blue marble sailed across the circle, hitting a black marble soundly and knocking it out. I scooped up the black marble and aimed again. Flick! A yellow one rolled out. Flick! Flick! A blue one, then a green one. There was only one marble left in the circle, an orange cat's-eye. I eyed it carefully. Flick! The blue marble flipped off my thumb, sped across the circle and knocked the cat's-eye marble out. I'd won my first marble game.

The buzzer sounded for the end of recess, and I stood up smiling. We spilled the marbles we'd collected back in the circle so everyone could collect their own. I put Old Blue down deep in my pocket.

"Nice job." Betsy smiled and gave me a pat on the back. "I thought you said you hadn't played much."

I shrugged. "Beginner's luck, I guess."

"Where'd you learn to play marbles like that?" Bobby hurried to catch up with me.

"Betsy taught me."

"She's not that good." Bobby's friendly blue eyes showed no trace of resentment. He nodded toward Ralph and Pete. "I don't think they liked you winning much."

Ralph scowled and shouldered a younger boy out of line. Pete squeezed in behind him, and the two lines followed Miss Jones up the stairs.

Chapter 7

The tap, tap of shoes in the hallway interrupted my concentration on the spelling words. When the door swung open, Miss Bailey smiled at the sight of all of us sitting at our desks and at least appearing to be studying. Miss Jones moved to the rear of the room and we could hear the murmur of their voices, although the words weren't decipherable. Then I caught my name, and I strained harder to hear, but they were whispering now.

"Matthew Freeman."

I jumped guiltily when Miss Jones spoke, although I didn't think I'd done anything wrong. "Yeah. I mean…yes, ma'am."

"Miss Bailey would like to speak to you. We will be dismissing school in ten minutes, so I will see you again tomorrow." She gave me a kind smile before she returned to the front of the classroom.

I followed Miss Bailey into the hall, and down the two flights of stairs to her office. She waved at the wooden chair facing her desk and swished her skirt around the file cabinet to her chair.

For a moment she just gazed at me, like I was a specimen in a lab. Then, leaning forward slightly across her desk, she spoke. "Matthew, we can find no record of a Lori Freeman living in Taylor Springs. There is no street named Canterbury Lane. There is no phone number matching what you gave us. I checked with the police in Taylor Springs, and they have no reports of missing boys, no listing of runaways. I checked with the police in Mitchellville and Petersburg. Neither of them have a listing for your mom, that phone number, or that street. I can be quite compassionate and understanding of difficult circumstances for children. But I cannot tolerate lying. And I have come to the conclusion that nothing you have told me is the truth."

She paused as if she were giving me a chance to confess. I studied a spot on the floor beneath her desk, trying desperately to figure out what to tell her.

"Matthew." Her voice was sharper now. "What can you tell me that will help?"

I raised my head and looked directly into her eyes. "I'm sorry, Miss Bailey. I can't remember anything except being in the field. Then I walked through the field to the Hawthornes. I think I have amnesia or something."

"Amnesia?"

"Yes. When I came to, I was lying on the ground. Maybe I hit my head or something."

She clasped her hands together in front of her, studying me again. "Why didn't you tell me this yesterday?"

"I was scared." That was the truth. And every minute I was in the orphanage, I'd become more scared—mostly that I would never see my family again.

"Amnesia," she repeated as if she were still mulling it over in her mind. "But there are still no reports of missing boys or runaways ... You couldn't have walked farther than Petersburg." She sighed heavily. "I guess for now you're our responsibility. I expect you to follow the rules and do as you're told."

I nodded politely. "Yes, ma'am, I will."

"I'll issue you some pants and shirts and underclothes. You don't need shoes do you?" She wrinkled her nose slightly as she looked at my 2016 pants and shirt.

I shook my head and stuck my feet out in front of me. "My shoes are good. They're great. They're Nikes."

"Nikes?" Miss Bailey shook her head. I didn't think she wanted me to explain, so I kept quiet.

She continued, "Mr. Garrett, the boy's staff leader, will explain our routine." Just the mention of his name made chills go up my arm.

She glanced at a large clock hanging on the wall. "You're dismissed to go upstairs. Do you remember the way to the boys' quarters?"

"Yes." I nodded at her as I stood up and hurried out of the room. I didn't know why I was so disappointed. I knew she wouldn't find my family in Taylor Springs in 1946, but I wanted her to find out something. I guess I was stuck here until the nightmare was over, or I could figure out how to get back on my own.

That night in the game room, as the others gathered to listen to the radio, I pulled out my blue marble and a few of the marbles on the shelf and practiced shooting from different positions. After a few shots, Bobby padded across the floor in his bare feet. He sat cross-legged to watch me.

"What did Miss Bailey tell you?"

I scooped up the marbles and returned all but my shooter to the can.

47

"No missing boys. No one is looking for me."

Bobby's forehead wrinkled as he thought. Then he hurried to the bedroom and came back with a small notebook and the stub of a pencil. "Let's write down everything we know. All the facts."

A few minutes later, his notebook said,

1. Woke up in Hawthornes' field
2. Has been in Taylor Springs before—recognized the library
3. Thinks he has a family somewhere

"Do you have a bump on your head or anything?" Bobby asked hopefully.

"No." I looked at the notebook. "We don't have much to go on. And we can't leave the Children's Home to look around. So what are we gonna do?"

"Hmmm." Bobby's forehead wrinkled. "I know. We can interview all the kids. See if there is anyone who has ever seen you. Sometimes we get to leave here—last summer we even got to go to a circus. Maybe someone saw you in Taylor Springs."

"Okay." I knew none of those kids had even been in Taylor Springs when I'd been there, but I couldn't tell Bobby that. He was so excited about finding my family.

Later, after we brushed our teeth and washed our faces, Bobby knelt beside his bed, his eyes closed and hands folded. I sat and watched. John and Lee walked past us toward the bathroom. I hoped Lee could keep his bed dry tonight.

Bobby climbed back up on his bed and sat cross-legged, facing me. His red hair stood up in every direction, but his eyes looked serious. "I pray every night that God'll give me a family. Now I ask Him to help you find yours, too."

What if you never get one? I wanted to ask, but I didn't.

As if he read my mind, Bobby continued. "Even if I never get another family, I know God loves me and gives me what's best. I remember my dad telling me that."

"What happened to your dad?"

Bobby's mouth puckered a little before he answered. "He was killed in the war."

"So was my dad," I whispered.

"You remember?" Bobby leaped off his bed, pulled out his basket, and found the little notebook. "What else?"

"His name was Richard..." My voice trailed off as if I couldn't remember. But I could. I remembered spending the day fishing, going for ice cream, wrestling on the living room floor, and reading adventure stories. And Dad always prayed with me at bedtime, his voice deep and low. I remembered so many things I never wanted to forget.

Bobby carefully printed "Richard" in the notebook and then, "Killed in the war."

I leaned over and whispered, "Does God hear you better if you kneel by the bed?"

Bobby closed the notebook and stretched way down to put it back under the bed. "Of course not, silly. God hears whatever we say, wherever we are, even our thoughts."

If God heard my thoughts, I was in big trouble.

Chapter 8

The whole world sounded different in 1946. There was no continual hum of computers, no cell phones ringing. The only phone was in Miss Bailey's office, and it had a softer buzzing ring. And my mom's voice wasn't the first voice of the morning.

Mr. Garrett yelled, "Everybody up!" I closed my eyes against the lights and listened to the thump of all the boys' feet hitting the cold, bare floor.

I groaned and rolled out, too. I didn't want Mr. Garrett to have any reason to notice me. My basket held some corduroy pants and a shirt like Bobby's, except mine was a blue plaid. I pulled on my clothes and thought about how Dusty would have laughed if he could have seen me in them. As I slipped into my Nike's and tightened the laces, Bobby's face appeared suddenly over my bed, peering down at me where I sat on the floor.

"There's another clue."

"What? Clue to what?"

"Finding your family. We could try to find where your funny-looking shoes came from."

"Yeah." I stood up. "Put that one in the notebook, too." And just how was he going to find that out? Google "Nike"? Not here. But somehow, it was comforting to know someone cared enough to try to get me back home.

In the kitchen, I could smell something baking. I sniffed in anticipation.

"Good morning, my handsome gentlemen." Jemma Jean pulled Benny to her in a hug, leaving a streak of flour from her apron across his cheek. One large hand ruffled Lee's hair. Her warm smile made us all feel as if we'd been the recipient of her hug.

"Frank, you be my stirrer. Ralph and Pete, I need you to set up the chairs. John and Lee can get the plates ready. Matthew, put the juice at each place." We hurried to do our duties without complaining.

I could hear the girls and younger children coming down the stairs as I put little glasses of juice on the table. When Betsy walked in, carrying the same little curly-headed girl, I gave a tiny wave. Betsy smiled and waved back. Then the line formed, and I went back in the kitchen to serve.

I helped Ralph as he split the warm biscuits I'd smelled and laid them on a plate for each child. As we finished he leaned over to me and whispered, "First recess, game just with older boys, playing for keepsies."

"I don't have any marbles of my own," I whispered back. "Just my shooter." My hand automatically dove into my pocket just to make sure it was still there.

"We'll loan you some. Just be there."

I didn't like to be told what to do, but I wanted to play marbles. Besides, Ralph was bigger than me, and I didn't want to make any enemies.

Later, in the classroom, I struggled to concentrate on the story. We took turns reading out loud about a girl whose biggest problem was choosing to be nice to another girl. It all seemed so old fashioned.

When math began, I groaned to myself. They were working on long division. I hadn't had that yet in 2016, and Miss Jones didn't have any calculators. Even if she did, she probably wouldn't let us use them. She was pretty strong on making us find our own answers.

Miss Jones finally asked Sharon to help me. But I couldn't follow what she was doing on my paper, and her long hair smelled like grease. It kept dragging across my arm as she leaned over my desk. I sighed with relief when Miss Jones finally announced, "Recess."

A large circle of boys gathered by the back fence. Ralph shouted orders at everyone. The circle in the dirt was larger than yesterday's, and the boys spread out around the edge, fingering their cloth bags of marbles. I wondered who would loan some to me.

"You can use these." Ralph dropped a small handful of marbles into my outstretched hand. They looked suspiciously like the ones from the can in the game room, but I didn't ask.

"Thanks." I stuffed them into the pocket opposite the blue marble.

"We'll do this like a tournament. If we don't finish before the bell, we'll keep going where we left off at the next recess. We'll do two groups, and the winners of both groups can play to determine the grand champion." He drew the word *champion* out, emphasizing all three syllables. "Pete and I will be the final judges because we're the oldest."

The Blue Marble

I watched as Pete drew the lag line. Ralph called the names of the boys who would be in the first game: Pete, Frank, Donovan, John, and Lee. He had chosen all the older boys, with the exception of Lee, who always shadowed his brother. Bobby, six-year-old Benny, Ralph, and I would play second. I settled back to watch.

The tosses from the lag line determined the order of players. Donovan played first. His first three shots netted him three marbles. After his fourth shot, he did a little dance around the edge of the circle. "Dubs!" he shouted as he pocketed two marbles that had both rolled out. When he shot the fifth time, his shooter rolled over the edge of the circle. He pushed his dark hair out of his eyes and, with a grin, joined those of us watching.

Pete shot next and won four marbles, John knocked out one, and Frank shot out two. Lee looked up at his brother before kneeling down to shoot. Despite intense concentration, he didn't knock out the last marble. Donovan took his second turn, shot the marble out, and won the game. He gave a friendly pat to Lee's shoulder. "You'll get one next time, buddy." Lee nodded without looking up.

Then our group stepped to the lag line and tossed out our marbles. Ralph would shoot first, then Bobby, me, and little Benny last. All of us dropped marbles out for the pot, a total of thirteen. Ralph arranged the cross, then swaggered to the edge of the circle and knuckled down. At the end of his turn, he'd pocketed four marbles. Bobby shot well and earned three.

I knelt at the edge of the circle with Old Blue. It spun off my index finger and knocked out a red marble. Green, black, and orange ones followed. I knelt for my fifth shot and aimed carefully at two marbles lined up near the edge. They were clear across the circle from my shooter. It would take a lot of speed and power to knock just one of them out. I took a deep breath and sent Old Blue on his way. Flick, click, click. The two marbles rolled out of the circle. I had a "dubs," and the game was over. I slipped the six marbles into my pocket.

When I stood up, grinning, I noticed that Ralph didn't look at all pleased. He motioned to the other boys. "Move back if you're just watching. We'll start the next game to see who's the champ-ee-on."

Donovan, Pete, and I would play again. But just as we lined up at the lag line, the bell rang.

"After school!" Pete shouted as we raced to make the neat line behind Miss Jones. As we marched into the building and up the stairs, I wondered where Betsy had been. She never missed a marble game.

Betsy wasn't at her desk behind Sharon in the classroom. I hoped she would be on the playground after school. She could see how well she'd taught me.

Despite Miss Jones's best efforts, the class buzzed about the marble game. Several people whispered, "Swell game" as they walked past my desk. After school, Mr. Garrett arrived and we lined up. Benny jostled to stand by me.

He tugged on my arm. "Will you teach me how to make a dubs?" His big brown eyes looked up at me imploringly.

"Sure! We fellas all need to stick together." I threw an arm around his shoulder. Like a punch in the stomach, a memory of Gabby surfaced.

She'd stood at the door of my room twirling her hair around her fingers. "Mattie, will you teach me how to ride the skateboard?"

"Are you kidding? Girls don't belong on skateboards. Go play with your dolls."

Guilt twisted like a snake through my belly, as I remembered how cruel I'd been to her.

After a meal of fried chicken which was even better than Mrs. Hawthorne's, we lined up behind Mr. Garrett and followed him outside.

We gathered around the marble circle, the crowd of boys larger than usual. Several girls even skipped across the playground to watch. I glanced around for Betsy, but she was still missing. We tossed marbles from a lag line to determine the order of play. Ralph would go first, then Donovan, and I would be last. That wasn't good. I might not even have a chance to shoot. Donovan and Ralph each dropped four marbles into the circle, I dropped in five. Ralph formed the cross, and then knuckled down with a frown of concentration.

His large purple shooter hit the cross with a smack, and several marbles scattered. He pocketed the green one which had rolled out. A red one, another green one, and an orange marble followed. He lined up with two "mibs" or targets on the opposite sides of the circle. But his marble rolled between them and out of the circle. I thought I heard him mutter a swear word as he backed up.

Donovan grinned, pushing his black curls off his forehead. "Here goes...perhaps the next champ-ee-on of the Taylor Springs Children's Home." He dropped to his knees and immediately sent his shooter sailing

56

after the marbles Ralph had missed. Click! One rolled out. Then he targeted the cluster of marbles still at the center. Another one rolled out. Two more shots, and two more marbles went in his pocket. He aimed his shooter at a white marble across the circle. Flick! The shooter rolled across, nudged the white one, and stopped. Donovan's turn was done.

I wiped my sweaty palms on my pants, wishing I had jeans on. I dug into my pocket for Old Blue. As I knuckled down, the circle of kids watching grew quiet. In order to win, I needed to get all five marbles. They were scattered around the circle.

I aimed for the red one first. Flick! Click! It rolled out, and my shooter stopped obediently inside the circle. I aimed for a black one, then a swirled orange. I pushed them down in my pocket. Next was a long shot for a green one. I got that one, too. My last shot was for a blue, swirly marble I knew belonged to Ralph. I took a deep breath, and aimed. Flick! Click! Out it rolled.

I threw a fist in the air and hollered, "Yes!" Kids crowded around, slapping my back and congratulating me on the win. I looked for Ralph to tell him, "Good game," but he'd slunk off to the far corner of the playground.

"Can I see your shooter?" Donovan's wide-open grin held no hint of jealousy. I handed him Old Blue, and he held it almost reverently, letting it rock around in his palm. "It never misses. Some taw!" He dropped it back in my palm, and I pocketed it just as the buzzer sounded to line up.

When I got into the boys' line, I found myself standing next to Sharon.

"Where's Betsy?" I didn't want to seem like I was looking for her, but I wondered why she hadn't watched the big tournament.

"She's been sick. I think they said she had a real high fever." Sharon gave me a shy smile. "I'll tell her you won the marble game."

I hoped Betsy would be better so she could watch me win the next one.

That night was shower night. We had to carry our clean pajamas down to the basement and wait for our turn in the showers.

Mr. Garrett handed us towels and gave a stern warning. "Wash behind your grubby, little ears, and I don't want to see any grimy fingers with dirt underneath the nails."

I looked for the shower stall, but it was just one long room with shower heads poking out every so often. The other boys stripped out of their clothes and scrubbed up under any available spot. I undressed slowly and slunk to a shower head at the end of the long room. I scrubbed a bar of hard, yellow soap on my washcloth and rubbed at the dirt on my elbows.

Later, Bobby and I sat on our beds, waiting for lights out. I'd emptied my pockets of marbles before we took our showers, and now I counted them.

"You were pretty amazing today," he said.

I held up Old Blue to the light, squinting at it and turning it to watch the patterns. "Must be Old Blue. He can't miss."

"My dad said not to trust in chariots."

"Huh?"

"In the Bible it says some trust in chariots, some trust in horses, but we trust in the name of the Lord."

"What does that mean?"

"That we only trust in God. That things and even people will let us down. But God won't."

"But…but…sometimes He doesn't do what we ask."

"Do you really believe God is real?"

I scratched my arm where the pajamas rubbed. "Yeah."

"Then you have to believe He will take care of us, and that He has a plan, even when He doesn't give us what we ask for."

"So do I ask God to help me win a marble game?"

"You can. And you can thank Him when you do win. But you can thank Him if you don't win, too. Because God always gives us His best, even when it doesn't seem like it. That's what trust is." Bobby gave me a lopsided grin as he slid off his bed and knelt. I knew he was asking God for a family. And asking Him to find mine.

Chapter 9

For the rest of the week, every recess was declared a "rematch" or a "new champion" tournament. And I never failed to win it. Even when Ralph cried, "Foul!" at several shots, I somehow managed to wind up with the most marbles. They quickly reinstated the "No Keepsies" rule, which was fine with me. I had added to the original six or seven marbles Pete gave me, and I now had a complete set. I traded for a cloth bag to keep them in, and somehow, with the bag in my pocket and Old Blue on top, I felt rich.

I hadn't seen Betsy. She must really be sick. I wondered what she did in bed all day. When I'd been sick, Mom had relented on the "one hour of screen-time" rule, and I'd gotten to watch TV or play games on her iPad. Unlimited electronics almost made being sick fun.

On Friday, I finally decided to ask Sharon again. "How's Betsy?"

She frowned and shook her head as Miss Jones looked our way. But when Miss Jones called up the fifth grade for reading, Sharon leaned over and whispered, "Betsy's fever's gone, but now she can't move her legs."

"Can't move her legs?" I echoed.

Sharon nodded. "I heard one of the nurses say something about polio."

Miss Jones looked up from her group. "Shhhhh."

Sharon ducked back to her work. I tried to remember what I knew about polio and wished for probably the millionth time that I could use a computer. Or ask my dad.

After reading, we took out some stories we had started yesterday about springtime. I raised my hand.

"Yes, Matthew?" Miss Jones stood by my desk.

"I want to find some more information for my story. Are there some kinds of books I could use?"

Miss Jones smiled. She seemed pleased by my interest. "We have a set of *World Book Encyclopedias.*" She pointed to the shelf by the window. "It's not the 1946 edition, but I'm sure you'll be able to find help for your topic."

I scooted over and found the book with a capital *P* on the cover. Flipping through the pages, I finally saw the page titled "Polio—Infantile Paralysis." There were a lot of terms in the article I didn't understand, but I learned that it was a virus, could be spread to others, and sometimes caused total paralysis or even death. The last sentence of the article said, "Doctors around the world are currently working on a vaccine that could reduce the devastation from polio epidemics."

A vaccine! That was where I had heard the word "*polio.*" Last year, when Mom took me to the doctor, I had to have some shots and one shot was so I wouldn't get polio. The vaccine must be effective, because I'd never known anyone with the disease. If that's what Betsy had, it was way more serious than just a cold or sore throat. I closed the encyclopedia and tried to push down the sick feeling rising inside me.

At recess, Donovan and Frank burst out of the door beside me. "Come on, Matt. The game's starting!"

I shook my head. "Go ahead and start. I'll just watch today." They tore off, and at the risk of being called "teacher's pet," I went to stand beside Miss Jones.

She smiled down at me. "Why, hello, Matthew. You're not playing marbles today?"

I shook my head. "Miss Jones, have you ever known anyone with polio?"

She raised an eyebrow. "Well, of course. I lost an uncle to polio when I was little. And my friend Kathleen contracted polio when she was a child. She walks with a cane. She was one of the lucky ones. Why do you ask?"

"I heard that might be what Betsy has."

A frown creased her brow. "I don't think she has a confirmed diagnosis yet. Are you worried about getting it? They moved Betsy to a room by herself."

"No, I'm not worried about catching polio."

"I'm sure the doctors and nurses who are taking care of Betsy are doing the best they can for her. You go on and play, and don't be concerned."

"Okay, Miss Jones." I wandered off toward the marble game. I could tell even from across the playground that Ralph was winning from the way he strutted around the circle.

Sharon was in line for the jump rope game. Taking the risk of being labeled both a teacher's pet and a girl-liker, I motioned her over.

With a quick "Hold my place" to the girl beside her, she jogged over, her stringy brown hair blowing across her smiling face. Cocking her head at me, she waited for me to talk first.

"I just wanted to know about Betsy."

Sharon's smile faded, and she gave a little shrug. "I already told you all I know. She was sick last week, running a fever and complaining that her throat hurt. They didn't even call the doctor, just made her stay in bed. Then she was feeling better, but now she can't lift her legs off the bed, and I heard the nurse say something about maybe she had polio. They moved her to the infirmary in the nurse's office, and I think the doctor is coming to look at her." Sharon looked over her shoulder to make sure it wasn't her turn.

"Thanks." I scuffed my feet through the dirt, deep in thought. I knew where the nurse's station was, across from Miss Bailey's office. I'd had to go there to see the doctor last Monday. He'd just taken my weight and height and looked at my ears and stuff. I guess they have to do that with every new boy to see if he's healthy.

When the buzzer sounded for the end of recess, I had a plan.

I let Miss Jones finish her explanation of the day's math and assign the page of problems we were to copy on our papers and solve. I carefully wrote my name in the corner of the page, along with the date. Then I raised my hand.

64

Miss Jones's shoes clicked their way to my desk. "Yes, Matthew? Do you need some help?"

"I have a headache." That wasn't a lie. Math always gave me a headache. "Could I go see the nurse for some Tylenol?"

"Tylenol?" she repeated, her forehead wrinkled in a frown.

"Aspirin, I mean."

She laid a cool hand on my forehead. "You don't seem to have a fever."

"Just a headache." I rubbed my temples. "I'm sure if I take an aspirin, I can finish these problems in no time."

"Well ..." She seemed to weigh my request. "I suppose so." She clicked back to her desk and filled out a tiny slip of paper which said "Hall Pass." Then she handed it to me. "I expect you to be back here in a timely fashion."

"Yes, ma'am." I scurried out the door, ignoring the curious glances from my classmates. I clattered down the narrow steps to the second floor and the wide steps to the first. Walking as quietly as I could, I looked through the glass in the door of Miss Bailey's office. She was busy typing. I waited until she looked down, and then I sped past her door.

The next door was the nurse's office. Nurse Cadie sat with her back to me, a book propped open on her desk. Beyond her was an open door. They'd put Betsy in that room, I was almost sure. But how to get past the nurse? The odd buzzing ring of the phone in Miss Bailey's office startled me, and then Miss Bailey's voice sounded over what must have been an intercom system. "Miss Cadie, you have a telephone call. Miss Cadie?"

I saw the nurse stand up and flip a switch on a small box on her desk. "Thanks. I'll be right there." She slid a bookmark between the pages of the book she was reading, laid it on the desk and with a glance toward the back door, stepped out in the hall. She gave a little start when she saw me. "Where'd you come from?"

I handed her the pass from my classroom. She took the paper without reading it and waved me into her office. "Take a seat. I'll be with you in a minute." Then she hurried across to Miss Bailey's office.

I ducked inside the hallway door, scooted around her desk and cabinet, and shoved open the connecting door to the back room. The shades were pulled over the window. I squinted in the dim light, trying to make out whether the still form on the bed was Betsy.

"Betsy?" I whispered.

Her head swiveled on the pillow to look at me. "Matthew, what are you doing here?"

"Came to see you." I took a couple of steps into the room. Betsy's hair was all wild, not in the neat braids she usually wore. Her face looked pale, even in the dim light, and her brown eyes were enormous.

"You can't be in here. I'm sick." Her hands clutched the piles of blankets tucked around her.

"I just wanted to tell you I'm hoping you get better so you can play marbles with us again."

"Thanks." A little smile twitched at the corners of her mouth. "I hate being sick." She made a movement like she was trying to sit up, but then a little moan came out, and her head flopped against the pillow. It was still hard to see, but it looked like there were tears in her eyes. "You better go."

I wanted to say something else, to tell her something that would give her hope.

"I'll ask God to help you get better," I whispered as I carefully closed the door again. I thought maybe I'd heard Betsy say, "Thanks" just as Nurse Cadie walked back in.

She glanced down at the pink hall pass I'd given her. "Have a headache, huh? Are you sure you're not giving Miss Jones a headache?" She chuckled at her own joke and reached for a large bottle of Bayer aspirin. She shook one tablet into her hand, then dropped it into mine and filled a small paper cup with water from the sink in her room. She watched as I swallowed the aspirin, then noted the time and scrawled her initials on the pass before giving it back to me. "Now get back to class."

That night in the game room, Bobby gave me a nudge and motioned me away from the group listening to *Amos 'n' Andy* on the radio. When we got to the shelf with the games he began to set up Uncle Wiggily.

"We don't really need to play. This is just a cover," he whispered, even though the others were clear across the room and engrossed in the program.

I sat across the board from him and put one of the little rabbits into the red stand. I hopped him randomly around the board. "What's up?"

"What's *up*?" He looked at me with a puzzled expression.

"What did you want to talk about?"

"Oh. Here's what we have so far." He opened his little notebook, and I could see he had filled several pages with names of the other kids who lived in the Children's Home. Beside their names he had written comments. "None of the other kids have ever seen you for sure. Two of them thought they might have seen you in Grayer's General Store, but they weren't positive. It could have just as easily been another kid with brown hair. It seems funny to me that no one has seen you, but you say Taylor Springs looks familiar."

I nodded. "I can show you where the courthouse is, the library—"

Bobby leaned over the board, knocking my little Uncle Wiggily figure over. "So here's my theory. You came from somewhere else and were just in Taylor Springs long enough so you remember those places."

"Maybe—"

"And if we can figure out where those crazy shoes of yours came from, maybe we could find out where *you* came from!" He finished with a flourish that scattered the red cards.

I tried to muster up some enthusiasm. Bobby was working so hard on finding where I'd come from.

"That's a great idea." I pasted a smile on my face.

"Listen to my plan. We get someone to take us to Grayer's. We look at the shoes there, talk to Mr. Grayer, and find out where you buy shoes like yours."

I certainly liked the part about going to Grayer's. Getting away from the Children's Home, even for only an hour or two, sounded wonderful.

68

"Who can we get to take us?" I glanced at Mr. Garrett. He leaned against the wall, frowning and watching Bobby and me.

"Not him!" Bobby blurted out. "I'll think of someone."

With a burst of laughter, the *Amos 'n' Andy* program ended, and Mr. Garrett announced, "Lights out in fifteen minutes."

Bobby and I scooped up the pieces of the Uncle Wiggily game and put them back in the box, folding the game board on top. We hurried to the bathroom, and then went to our beds.

Bobby knelt immediately. I knew he would pray that his plan would work and that we'd find my family.

I took a deep breath and slipped off my bed and onto my knees. "It's been a long time, God. But this isn't about me. Please, just help Betsy to get better."

Chapter 10

I woke up early needing to use the restroom. I slid out of bed and padded through the dark room to the bathroom. John was there helping Lee out of some very wet pajamas. He glanced up at me and then held out his arm for his brother to grab as he stripped off the bottoms.

"What are you going to do with those?" I pointed to the pile of wet things.

"If I hide them at the bottom of the dirty clothes, most times no one notices. But the sheets are the worst. If I just make the bed, they don't dry. If I leave them out, then he sees them."

There was no need for him to specify who "he" was. At that moment the bedroom flooded with light, and Mr. Garrett's harsh voice boomed out. "Boys, up! All you little worms, up and out." I helped John stuff the clothes into the bottom of the basket and hurried into the bedroom as the rest of the boys scrambled to get to the bathroom. Pulling on my clothes, I tried to ignore the sick feeling inside. I didn't think I could watch Lee or John get strapped for wetting the bed. But what could I do?

Mr. Garrett returned as I pulled the laces tight on my Nikes. I looped and tugged, and then bounced to my feet as he strode between the rows of beds. When he reached Lee's bed, he paused, then continued down the row. I let out my breath.

Then he turned on one heel and stepped back to the bed. Pulling back the covers, he shook his head. "I thought I was in the older boys' room, but I must have gotten into the babies' room by mistake." His hand snaked out and grabbed Lee by his shirt. Lee's face went white, and his eyes filled with tears, but he didn't say anything.

"Bend over," Mr. Garrett commanded as he raised the leather strap.

A hot anger surged through me. "No!" I shouted. "It was me. Lee and I traded beds last night, 'cause … 'cause …'cause Bobby snores."

Mr. Garrett raised his head to look at me, but he didn't release his hold on Lee.

"That's not true!" Bobby vaulted over his bed to stand beside me. "I was the one who traded beds with Lee."

On the other side of the room, I heard the boys moving restlessly. Then Donovan stepped across the room. For once, he wasn't grinning. He pushed at the dark curls on his forehead. "I traded beds with Lee last night. It was me."

One by one, Frank, John, and Pete claimed they had wet the bed. Finally, Mr. Garrett's grip on Lee's shirt loosened, and Lee fled into his brother's arms.

"Okay. If that's how you want to play it …" He popped the strap against his palm and uttered a little sound that sounded like a snarling dog. "Maybe I should strap all of you. Maybe I will. But for now, no outdoor time after supper. No *Amos 'n' Andy.* Everyone will be in bed at seven until further notice, or until,"—he gave a mean look to Lee—"the boy who did sleep here steps forward."

Despite the punishment, all the way down to the kitchen I felt as warm and toasty inside as the steaming pancakes that awaited us.

For a while, all the boys seemed united in the common victory. We hustled into the kitchen, eager to please Jemma. As I sat down at the table with my stack of pancakes, syrup dripping off the edges, I felt pretty smug, like a champ-ee-on.

Ralph scooted in next to me. "So what now, Matthew? You gonna tell Garrett that you wet Lee's bed and take a lickin' for him, or are you just gonna let us miss outdoor time forever?"

Suddenly my pancakes didn't taste so sweet. I hadn't thought that far ahead. How would we be able to win back our free time without someone getting strapped? "I'll figure out something." I forked another bite in and chewed slowly.

"Well, you better figger it out quickly. I don't like missin' outdoor time."

The girls were finishing their breakfast as we stuffed the first bites in our mouths. I was licking syrup off a finger when Sharon leaned down and whispered, "Betsy is back in the bedroom. They carried her up last night."

"Great!" I smiled up at her, but Sharon didn't return the smile.

"She can't move her legs. She's paralyzed."

I swiveled in my seat as Sharon moved toward the kitchen with her plate. "She'll get better, won't she?"

Sharon's brown hair hid her face as she shrugged. "Nobody knows."

It didn't seem fair. I'd tried to do what Bobby had said, to trust in God, but now I had lost outdoor time for everyone, Betsy couldn't move her legs, and I still had no clue how to get back to my family in 2016. And I wanted to be there more than ever.

It clouded up and rained in the afternoon. I don't think I've ever been so happy to see raindrops splashing on the windows. Now, no one could be angry at me for missing outdoor time.

We wandered around the game room before supper; no one seemed to be able to find anything to do. I wished I could sneak over to the girls' dormitory to see how Betsy was doing, but I knew the consequences of being found there would be even more severe than claiming to wet a bed.

Frank made a circle with a piece of string, and I joined the group to play a game of marbles. No one really seemed to have his heart in it. I won easily, but felt no thrill from the victory. When Mr. Garrett announced it was time to line up for supper, we spilled all the marbles back into the circle, and everyone collected his own, since we no longer played for keepsies. Bobby scooted to the line ahead of me. He had his notebook, filled with clues to help us find my family, tucked into his back pocket. I wondered why he was taking it with him to supper.

I slid onto the bench, balancing my plateful of chicken and noodles on the tray. I couldn't wait to dig in. I looked around for Bobby. He'd been ahead of me, but he was nowhere to be seen. What was he up to now? I didn't have to wait long to find out. He slipped onto the bench beside me, bumping my arm and spilling some of my bottle of milk. It dribbled down my chin and splashed onto my shirt.

"Hey!" I dabbed at my shirt with my napkin.

Bobby was breathless with excitement. He didn't even apologize for spilling my milk. "Guess what? Jemma said she would take us to Grayer's next Saturday. And she'll help us look at all the shoes and talk to Mr. Grayer, and we get to go with her, and it will be just us two!"

Even though I knew looking at shoes in Grayer's General Store in 1946 couldn't get me back to my family in 2016, I felt a surge of enthusiasm. "No kidding? She's going to take us?"

"Well, she has to talk to Miss Bailey and get it all approved, but she didn't think anybody would mind."

The whole possibility of finding my family seemed to set Bobby's mind to racing. And in between huge mouthfuls of chicken and noodles he quizzed me about Mom and Gabby, writing my answers in the notebook in his loopy cursive writing.

And I sat wondering, would I ever see them again?

Chapter 11

For a moment, every jump rope stopped, the marble game ceased, and even the swings halted. It was as if someone had pushed a pause button on the playground. Nurse Cadie held the door as Miss Bailey maneuvered a wheelchair outside. Betsy gripped the armrests as it bounced over the threshold onto the playground. She wore one blanket draped around her shoulders, another tucked over her legs. Her face looked pale, but a smile lit up her face like sunshine poking through the clouds.

Immediately, girls surrounded the chair, giggling, pushing, and vying for the chance to say hello. I stood by the oak tree, waiting my turn at the marble game.

Frank nudged me. "You gonna play marbles or stare at the girls?"

I elbowed him back and knelt to take my turn. But after shooting, I looked at Benny. "You want to play my next turn?"

He nodded eagerly. "Sure!"

Then, knowing I would be teased for the next few days, I wandered over to Betsy. Most of the girls had gone back to their jump ropes or jacks. Only Sharon stood there, having been granted the privilege of pushing the chair. There wasn't much place to go. Only a small area had a sidewalk, and it was crowded with jump ropes. But Sharon kept a tight grip on the handles anyway.

"Hey, Betsy." I pretended I was just walking by.

"Hi, Matthew." Her face blossomed into a wide smile. "Still winning all the marble games?"

"Yep." I pulled my shooter out. "Old Blue never fails me."

Her smile faded a little. "Not sure when I can play again."

"Can…can you move your legs yet?"

She shook her head, looking down at her lap. One hand picked nervously at the blanket. "I have some feeling back, but everything is floppy. Dr. Jeffries said I don't have any muscle strength. If I could get some leg braces, I might be able to walk, but no one has any money to get them. So"—she looked up at me and tried to smile again—"I'm stuck in this chair."

"Well …" I glanced across the playground, half-expecting to see a whole gang of boys, pointing at me and laughing.

"Go on, win a game for me." She waved me off.

I hesitated. Then with a quick wave, I jogged back to the marble circle, just in time for my turn, but I let Benny take it anyway. I couldn't believe someone who needed leg braces couldn't get them just because they were an orphan. It didn't seem right.

I talked to Bobby about Betsy that night. Although we still had the seven o'clock bedtime, Mr. Garrett didn't seem to notice or care if we talked as long as we didn't get out of our beds.

"Isn't there someone who could buy the braces for her? A charity of some sort?"

Bobby's freckled face wrinkled as he thought. "I don't know who. Jemma said all of the country's money went to pay for the war. Here at the Children's Home, we're just lucky we get fed and clothed."

"How much would braces cost?"

I could hear his cheeks puffing out air. "I don't know. Way more than you or I have."

"There's got to be a way to get the money."

"How? There's no way to earn anything in here. We can't sell newspapers or run errands. Let's talk about it tomorrow, okay?" Bobby yawned.

"Maybe we should pray about it. Didn't you say God provided for our needs? I think Betsy needs those braces."

I heard Bobby roll over and sigh. "You're right, Matthew. Do you think Mr. Garrett would catch us if we got out of bed?"

"Do we have to get out of bed? Doesn't God see and hear us wherever we are?"

"Yeah," Bobby answered slowly, like he was thinking about it.

So I just prayed, whispering the words. "God, Betsy needs braces. We don't know how to get them for her, and she doesn't have any money. And we'll help however You need us to."

I heard Bobby's steady whisper. "I'll help, too, God. Betsy needs those braces. Amen."

From across the aisle, I heard Donovan's voice. "Me, too, God. Amen."

Then up and down the rows of beds, I heard boys' voices. They were all praying that Betsy would get her braces. I leaned back against my pillow with a smile. I didn't know how He would do it, but I was trusting God for something Big.

Chapter 12

Two weeks later, nothing had happened. Absolutely nothing.

"Maybe God didn't hear us," I told Bobby.

"He heard. God always hears. Sometimes we just have to wait."

"Well," I grumbled, "I don't think it's quite fair to keep Betsy waiting." It hurt to watch her just sitting in that chair. Before polio, Betsy had been the first girl on the playground. She was a great marble player, she could do all the jump rope moves, and she'd taught the little girls how to turn cartwheels and to use their legs to pump the swings. At breakfast, she'd carried the babies on her hip, toting them around and feeding them cereal. Now she watched others doing the things she used to. She kept a smile on her face, but I thought her eyes looked sad.

Bobby and I sat on the bench outside Miss Bailey's office, swinging our legs and waiting for Jemma Jean. I was excited to go to Grayer's just to get away from the orphanage for a couple hours. Bobby couldn't stop talking about finding my mom. He had his notebook ready and kept adding to his list of questions for the owner of the store, Mr. Grayer.

"We'll ask him if he's ever seen you…and if he sells shoes like yours…and who bought shoes like them…and…"

Miss Bailey walked out of her office with Jemma Jean. I'd never seen our cook in anything but a print dress and her flour-covered apron. Now she wore a light-green, silky dress and a kind of perky, little hat with feathers that matched the color of her dress. White-gloved hands clutched the handle of a shiny, black purse.

"Wow! You look pretty, Jemma," I said.

Miss Bailey frowned at me. "Mrs. Foster, Matthew."

I studied the toe of my Nikes. I'd never even heard Jemma Jean's last name. "I'm sorry."

"Ready to go, boys?" Jemma didn't seem to mind that I'd called her by her first name. Her wonderful, bright smile covered her face.

"I expect you two to mind your manners!" Miss Bailey called as we trotted off down the hall.

Jemma didn't have a car, so we followed her to a bench at the end of the block and waited for the bus. We didn't have to wait long for the funny-looking vehicle. Rods on the roof of the bus hooked to cables, which crisscrossed above the streets. Jemma took both of us by the hand, and we walked to the middle of the street. The bus waited, the electric arms waving like a space creature with antennae.

Jemma opened her purse with a gloved hand and removed three coins, giving one to Bobby and me. I watched Bobby drop his coin through the slot into the container behind the driver. I dropped mine in, too, and it fell with a little clunk. Then we walked past the men in suits and ladies in hats to the back of the bus, where a long bench stretched from one window to the other. Bobby and I sat on either side of Jemma.

The bus bounced along the street, the cables overhead humming a tuneless song. We turned a couple corners, and then Jemma stood and pulled on a cord. Squeaking to a stop, the doors opened with a swish, and

Bobby and I followed Jemma out, leaping off the last step.

Downtown Taylor Springs rose all around us, tall brick buildings with wide glass windows in front. All the cars and trucks were black, and they chugged slowly up and down the streets, occasionally backfiring with a loud bang. People strolled on the sidewalks, most of them dressed like they were going to a party, the women in dresses with fancy hats and gloves and the men in suits with felt hats. A few stone buildings seemed familiar, but most looked like a scene from one of my grandma's books.

We walked about a block and pushed open a glass door into Grayer's General Store. A little bell tinkled as the door opened. I stepped inside and blinked for a few minutes as my eyes adjusted from the bright sunlight outside to the dim interior. Food smells mingled with the scents of leather, new fabrics, and tools, all blending together in a musty, dusty odor that reminded me of the attic in my great-aunt Charlotte's house. Floor-to-ceiling shelves held every imaginable object. Toys were stacked next to kitchen items which were piled beside hammers and shovels.

In 2016, Grayer's was a well-lit hardware store, with mostly tools on their shelves. Dad had taken me there before he was deployed.

Jemma turned to us. "You boys stay right here with me. We'll do the shopping I need to do first; then we'll look at the shoes. You know what you want to ask him?"

Bobby nodded confidently. "Got it all in here." He patted his pocket bulging with the outline of his notebook.

Jemma walked slowly up and down the aisles of the store, fingering the fabric on the sleeves of a rack of new dresses, lifting a lid to inspect a pan, and stooping to sift through small packages of garden seeds. Bobby and I did our own gawking at a selection of heavy, fat-tired bicycles, shiny new scooters way bigger than Dusty's sister's, and a long glass counter filled with bins overflowing with candy.

Finally, Jemma shifted her bag and smiled down at us. "Okay, now. Let's go look at the shoes."

In the very rear of the store were three wooden chairs surrounded by stacks of shoe boxes. As soon as we sat, a thin man in a white shirt and suspenders approached. His long, droopy mustache moved up and down as he spoke. "What handsome young gentlemen you have with you today. And what would you like to look at? Some sturdy Buster Browns for school? Maybe some Sunday shoes?"

"The boys here want to ask some questions. They're looking for someone."

A puzzled frown caused the mustache to droop even farther. "I just sell shoes here."

Bobby pointed to my Nikes. "Do you sell any shoes like these?"

"Hmmmm." The man knelt down to look, taking my foot in his hand and turning it this way and that. He touched the swoosh emblem on the side. "Never seen a shoe like this in my life. Strange. I can't even tell what material it's made out of." He read the Nike label on the tongue, but he said the word in one syllable, rhyming with *bike*. "Where in the world did you get shoes like this, boy?"

Somewhat embarrassed, I tucked them under my chair. "My mom bought them."

84

Bobby wiggled forward. "We're from the Children's Home and he has amnesia and he can't find his mom, but he knows he's been in Taylor Springs and we thought we might be able to trace something through his shoes." The words poured out as if he thought by saying everything real fast, the man would agree to help.

Shaking his head, the man stood. "I wish I knew something. But Grayer's doesn't sell shoes like those. I know my shoes, and I don't think any place in Missouri sells shoes like that."

"Have you ever seen him?" Bobby pointed to me.

"There's a lot of boys come in here every day. Can't say as I remember this one specifically."

Bobby drooped lower than the mustache. I tried to catch his eye, smile at him, and tell him it was okay, but his head was down.

Jemma stood up and held out a hand to each of us. "Well, come along boys." She nodded to Mr. Grayer. "Thanks for talking with them."

At the front of the store, Jemma laid her purchases on a wooden counter. The cashier opened a shiny, black cash register and punched in numbers by hand. She told Jemma the total and Jemma carefully counted it out, putting the dollars and change in the cashier's hand. Then she gestured to the candy, "Go ahead and pick out a penny's worth each."

"Thanks!" we both chorused and pressed our faces to the glass, trying to make the difficult choice. I hoped the candy would cheer Bobby up. I sidestepped down the counter, looking at the piles of round yellow, red, and brown candies. I couldn't believe how much candy you could buy for a penny.

"What do those taste like?" I pointed to the brown ones.

Bobby looked at the bin I indicated. "Root beer. Those are root beer barrels."

"And those?" I moved to the round red ones.

"Cinnamon balls. They're hot! Haven't you had candy before?"

"Well, yeah, I've had candy. Just not like these. I like Nerds and Starburst and Sour Patch Kids."

Staring at me like I was an alien, Bobby started to reach for his notebook, but then he turned his attention back to the candy. My odd candy choices could wait.

I moved on down. I was just about ready to decide between the root beer barrels and some chocolates when a flyer taped on the front of the case caught my eye.

National Marble Tournament
Taylor Springs, Missouri
May 4, 1946
Anyone can enter, 25 cent entry fee
Calling all marble champions, come try your luck against the best!
$100 Grand Prize

At the bottom "Registration forms available at the cash register" was penciled in. I read it through twice, patting my pocket once, just to make sure Old Blue was there. "Jemma, Bobby, look at this!" I hopped in excitement as they both came over.

Bobby read it, shaking his head. "Miss Bailey would never approve a pass to do this. And where would you get the twenty-five cents for the entry fee? We don't have any money."

86

"Maybe I could sell my shoes. Jemma, will you help us? I know that twenty-five cents is a whole lot more than a penny, but if you would pay the entry fee, instead of buying me candy, and if Miss Bailey would let me enter, I know I could win. And look, the grand prize is a hundred dollars. I bet that would be enough to buy those braces for Betsy." My words tumbled out of my mouth like marbles from a cloth bag.

"Whoa, slow down, son." Jemma rummaged in her purse and pulled out some glasses. She put them on, perching them on the end of her nose. Then she bent forward to read the flyer, using her finger to trace under the words, whispering them out loud.

"National Marble Tournament…anyone…twenty-five cents…grand prize."

She removed the glasses and looked at me. "You think you have a chance against boys from all across this country?"

I nodded. "I think I can do it. I have my blue marble."

"And you want to use the prize money to buy braces for that little girl in pigtails that got polio?"

"If she had braces, she might learn to walk. She hates being in that chair all the time."

Jemma folded the glasses and put them back in her purse. Then she tugged at the ends of her gloves. Finally, she laid a warm hand on my shoulder and looked at me. "I'll talk to Miss Bailey."

She looked over at Bobby. "Can he play marbles?"

"Yeah. He's the best."

Looking back at me, she smiled. "Well, son, you got two weeks to practice up. You better be the best if you're gonna get those braces for Betsy. Now," she said, moving toward the cash register, "you get your candy picked out, 'cause we're here at Grayer's, and I'm buying candy today."

On the return trip in the streetcar, I sucked on a root beer barrel. Three more candies were in a white paper bag stuffed in my pocket. And in my hand I clutched a registration form for the National Marble Tournament.

Chapter 13

Now, you just put that registration in your pocket," Jemma warned me as we walked up the steps of the Children's Home. "You let me talk to Miss Bailey first about this before you announce to the world that you're gonna be in a marble tournament. That don't mean you can't be a-practicing. Just keep it on the hush-hush until Miss Bailey decides."

"I will, Jemma." I folded the paper carefully and tucked it deep in the pocket where I kept my blue marble. Then, I held open the door for her and Bobby to walk through. "And thanks for taking us to Grayer's. I had a great time, even if we didn't find my mom."

Jemma smothered me in a hug. "You just wait, honey chile. I think your mama's gonna show up. You're a special boy, and I know she's looking for you."

Bobby gave Jemma a hug, too. Then we heard the click of Miss Bailey's shoes down the hall.

"Welcome back, boys. I believe your group is outside for recreation. You may join them."

It had been two weeks since we'd regained outdoor time from Mr. Garrett, and it still seemed like a treat. We scooted down the hall and out the door as Miss Bailey and Jemma talked in low tones behind us. I wondered whether Jemma would ask her today about the tournament or if I would have to wait.

As we stepped onto the playground, the other children swarmed around us like bees at a hive, buzzing with questions about our day. "Did Grayer's have any new scooters for sale?" "Were the Radio Flyer wagons out yet?" "Did you buy a pack of baseball cards?" "Did you find your mother, Matthew?"

"Hold on guys, we can only answer one question at a time." Bobby held up his hands, palms out. "We didn't find his mom exactly, but we got some more clues." Bobby patted his notebook and nodded in a mysterious way. "That's all we can say about it now, but we'll let you know as soon as we can."

The kids began buzzing again, but just then the bell rang, and we jostled for our places in line for lunch. Since Jemma had been gone with us in the morning, the older girls, under the supervision of their staff leader, had fixed sandwiches. We got our plates and made our way to the tables.

It seemed that Bobby and I were the most popular boys in the lunch room, with everyone crowding and shoving to sit near us. Bobby launched into a detailed account of the trip, and I sat and listened, trying to remember when one of my friends in 2016 had been excited by a trip to the store, especially if the only thing purchased for them had been a penny's worth of candy.

Saturday afternoon was visiting time. Some of the kids, especially the younger ones, weren't actually orphans; their parents had just been unable to care for them. So they'd brought them to the Children's Home and left them. But they came to visit and offered hope that someday they would all be able to live together again.

Donovan's parents were dead, but he had an uncle who came to visit him every Saturday. Little Benny's mom and dad visited him, but not every week. Occasionally, a couple would come, wanting to adopt a child. Almost always, they picked one of the babies or very young children. Except for the children who had visitors, the day was a sad reminder that we had no family. And even though I thought about my mom and Gabby every day, on Saturdays I felt like an orphan.

Bobby and I joined Frank and John in a game of Monopoly, but we played without much interest. After a while I went bankrupt, so I wandered over to a corner of the room, sat on the edge of the rug and practiced shooting marbles. I was learning exactly where and with how much force to hit a marble with Old Blue and to make it go the direction I wanted.

I took careful aim, practicing for "dubs" or two marbles out with one shot, when a shadow passed over Old Blue. I looked up into Mr. Garrett's scowling face.

"So you fancy yourself a marble player, huh?" His tone was mocking.

I didn't know how to answer him and keep myself out of trouble. "Ummm, I like to play marbles. I practice a lot. It's okay, isn't it?" I sat back on my heels and looked up at him with what I hoped was an innocent smile.

"Well, Mr. Marble Player, I just want you to know. Your little trick of covering for that baby bed wetter isn't going to work again." His eyes narrowed as he glared at me. "I will strap the lot of you next time." He turned on his heel and sauntered across the room.

I scooped up my marbles and dropped them back in their cloth bag. I didn't feel much like practicing anymore.

How could we protect Lee? With the threat of a strapping, no one would stand up for him. If we could just do something that would help him stop wetting the bed.

I still puzzled over this dilemma as I bit into the large piece of meatloaf Jemma had dished onto my plate for supper. I used the straw to suck up the last of my milk. If I was still thirsty, I could get a glass of water from the kitchen, but I usually didn't bother.

That was it! I leaned over to Donovan, sitting to my right and whispered, "If you want to help Lee, drink all your milk and as much water as you can hold. Pass it on."

He looked up at me and wrinkled his brow, but as I went to the kitchen for water, I saw him lean over to Frank and pass the message down the table. One after another, Donovan, Frank, Bobby, and John got up and went to the kitchen. Up and down the table, raised eyebrows and questioning looks were directed at me. I just shook my head at them.

Mr. Garrett usually left our bedroom as we were getting our pajamas on, and then he turned up after about ten minutes, sometimes smelling like cough medicine. We never wanted to get him upset, so there were few problems we didn't solve ourselves. I waited until I heard his footsteps echo down the upstairs hall toward his room.

I motioned everyone over. "Here's the plan. If we drink all we can, most of us will have to get up in the night to pee. If we have to get up, we get Lee up, too. That way Lee will go several times in the night and will be dry in the morning. What do you guys think?"

"I ain't takin' a chance of a lickin' to help no bed wetter." Ralph went back to his bed, with Pete following.

I wasn't deterred; I figured they wouldn't participate anyway. "How about the rest of you? Are you in?"

Donovan, Frank, Bobby, John, and Benny all nodded. Lee just looked apprehensive.

"He ain't easy to wake up," John warned us.

"We'll get him up." Donovan nudged Lee. "Even if we have to stand the bed on end so he slides out in a pile on the floor." Lee smiled up at him but, as always, didn't speak.

I turned to Benny and used a technique Mom had used with Gabby and me when she didn't think we were old enough to do something. "Benny, I know you want to help. But I think we should wait until you're in second grade. When you're in second grade, you can get Lee up in the night."

He nodded cheerfully. "Okay!"

That left five of us. "Let's see how it goes for a couple nights. Then maybe we could split up the nights."

We heard footsteps and scattered like marbles hit by a heavy shooter. "What's going on? You boys plotting something?" Mr. Garrett snarled.

"No sir." Bobby always showed respect, even if the person wasn't exactly deserving of it.

"Pete! What's going on in here?"

"Aww, they was just talking about getting up at night to pee."

Mr. Garrett glared at us. "The light's on in the bathroom if anyone needs to use it. Just like always. Now, no more congregating. Get in those beds." We scrambled to our beds and barely made it before he barked, "Lights out. And no talking." He turned on his heel, flipped off the switch, and left the room.

For a few minutes, there wasn't a sound, not even the creak of a bedspring as someone turned over. We seemed frozen in place.

Then John whispered, "Thanks, everyone." And suddenly the room was full of whispering as we settled in. I no longer needed Bobby to remind me. I had lots to pray about. I slid out of bed and got on my knees.

"God, let Miss Bailey see that I need to play in the Nationals and get the braces for Betsy. Help me to wake up so I can get Lee to the bathroom. And somehow send me back to my family. Amen."

Chapter 14

Several of us yawned and stumbled as we made our way to the bathroom the next morning. Across the room John wore a huge smile. He made a circle with his thumb and forefinger—an "okay" sign—and nodded at me. Then, as I turned to go wash up, Lee skidded across the room and wrapped both arms around me in a huge hug.

I patted his blond curls. "You're welcome, buddy." And then, with a sickening twist in my stomach, I remembered once when Gabby had tried to hug me, and I'd shoved her hard enough to push her down. And then I laughed when she cried.

As we pulled on our shirts and pants, I asked Bobby, "How do you tell God you're sorry for things you've done?"

He laughed. "You say, 'I'm sorry.'"

I sighed. I needed a long time to tell God all the things I was sorry for.

Jemma was stirring a steaming pot of oatmeal as we filed in. She let Pete take over the stirring, and then, with a little pat or a hello, she put each of us to work. I buttered the thick slices of oven-toasted bread.

"Tell me, Matthew, was the meatloaf too spicy last night?" Jemma pulled another sheet of toast out of the oven.

"No. Not at all. It was great."

"Well, I noticed that several of you came to the kitchen for water." She looked down at me with her warm brown eyes.

Maybe it wouldn't hurt to have an adult in on the plan. I looked to see if Mr. Garrett was around. He sat in the dining room near the doorway, eating his breakfast in huge bites. Couldn't wait to leave us, I bet.

I spread butter on another slice. "Lee wets the bed. And then Mr. Garrett straps him. So we're trying to drink enough so we have to get up in the night. Then, whoever gets up, takes Lee to the bathroom, too. It worked last night."

"I see." Jemma gave me a little hug. "Well, I'm glad to hear it's not my cooking. I'll keep handing out the glasses of water."

The following Monday, we'd just started math when Miss Bailey walked in. Immediately, Miss Jones went to the back of the room. I kept my pencil busy, but I watched them out of the corner of my eye. I could hear them whispering. Every so often one of them looked in my direction, so I figured the discussion involved me. A tiny sprout of hope that somehow Miss Bailey had found my mom wiggled its way to my heart. I pictured my mom waiting downstairs on the hard bench outside Miss Bailey's office. I imagined hugging her and asking about Gabby.

"Matthew, Miss Bailey would like to visit with you," Miss Jones said.

I nearly tripped jumping out of my desk to follow her out into the hall.

Miss Bailey waited until I stood still before she spoke. "Mrs. Foster tells me that you want to enter a tournament for marble players."

The image of my mom slowly faded. "Yes, ma'am, I do. It's in Taylor Springs."

"Do you know the date?"

"Saturday, May fourth."

96

"And what would be the purpose of going to this tournament?"

I looked down at the floor and scuffed my toe on the worn wooden floor. "If I won, I could buy braces for Betsy."

Miss Bailey waited until I raised my eyes. "That's a very noble gesture, young man." She paused as if she wanted me to respond, but I didn't know what to say. "We've decided that this would be a good activity for a group of boys. We happened to receive a donation for an outing from the Elks Club, and I plan to approve your request. Do you think there are others who would like to enter?"

"Yeah! There are about ten of us who play marbles every recess."

"I'm not sure we can send all ten of you, but a group of five would be manageable. I will make an announcement after school this afternoon. Let's just keep quiet about it until then. Can you do that, Matthew?"

"You bet." I drew my thumb and index finger across my lips to show they were zipped. This wasn't as good as finding Mom and Gabby, but it was still good.

When I walked back into the classroom, heads turned, eyes peeped over books, and pencils stilled. The air was heavy with questions, but I didn't even look directly at anyone. I slid into my seat and tried to focus on the math problem I'd been working on earlier. Later, I stole a look at Betsy, sitting across the room in her wheel-chair, and tried to imagine her running across the playground again.

Chapter 15

Miss Bailey cleared her throat. "The board of directors of Taylor Springs Children's Home decided to allow five boys to enter the National Marble Tournament. Your registration will be paid by a generous donation."

For a nanosecond the room fell silent, and then everyone talked at once. It sounded more like a classroom in 2016 than the quiet room I'd gotten used to. Hands shot into the air and waved with questions for Miss Bailey.

Ralph spoke first. "How will they choose which boys get to go?"

Miss Bailey waited a moment until the class got quiet. "For those who want to enter, preference will be given to the older boys. However, if anyone gets a detention or misdemeanor, they will automatically be disqualified."

Sharon's long arm shot up. "Can the girls watch?"

"I'm not sure. Perhaps it would be a suitable outing. We'll make that decision when it gets closer to the date."

Frank asked for all of us, "How do we sign up?"

"I'll let Mr. Garrett know about the tournament, and as soon as we get registration forms, he can hand them out. You will be responsible to fill out the required information and return them to me. I'll make sure the form and the entry money get submitted."

I groaned inwardly. If Mr. Garrett knew we really wanted to go, he was sure to make things difficult.

Beginning that afternoon, the marble games became more intense. As soon as we were released for recess, the circle for the game was drawn and the players were organized. There was less joking and more concentration as we knuckled down for our shots.

The boys who weren't entering the competition either watched or played marbles in a different area of the playground. John chose not to enter. I think he knew Lee would panic if his brother left him for the day, and since Lee was the second youngest in our group, we knew he wouldn't be chosen. Benny wanted to enter and cried when Ralph told him he was too little.

After supper that night, Ralph asked Mr. Garrett if he had the registration forms. He acted like he knew nothing about them.

"No one told me about a marble tournament. You mean, they're going to let some of you worms go to the Cheyenne County fairgrounds for the entire day to play marbles? I'm not taking any of you. I don't get paid enough for that. Go on, listen to the radio. I don't have any forms. Not sure I'd give them to you if I had them."

Ralph persisted, and three days later when he asked, Mr. Garrett pulled some folded papers from his pocket. "Here they are. I'm not helping any of you. I want nothing to do with it. And I'll be watching ... One detention and you're out of the tournament."

100

There were five forms with the names already filled in: Ralph, Pete, Donovan, Frank, and Matthew. These were the five oldest boys who wanted to enter. I looked at Bobby. The freckles on his nose seemed to stand out even more. My best friend wouldn't be going with me.

"It's okay," he said. "I knew I wouldn't be able to go. You just go and win for all of us."

We filled out the registration forms the best we could, ignoring the line that asked for "Name of Parent." Then we gave them to Miss Jones the next morning to take to Miss Bailey. We didn't trust Mr. Garrett to get them to her.

Every chance we got, we worked on our strategies and improving our games. Ralph and Pete talked constantly about what they were going to do with the prize money when they won.

"Just may buy me a ticket to Californy." Ralph strutted around the circle.

Pete finished his shot and looked up. "Naw, I'd buy things. Maybe my very own radio." His eyes looked dreamy as if he could actually see it. I thought of my iPod, TV, and game system in my bedroom in 2016. Shaking my head, I tried to concentrate on my current world and on using Old Blue to knock two marbles out at once.

Donovan waited until I'd taken my shot, then nudged me. "What would you buy, Matthew?"

I shrugged. "Gotta win before we can get the prize money." I knelt for my next shot, and it grew quiet around the circle.

That night, everyone seemed a bit on edge. Frank and I played Monopoly. When I landed on his Park Place property, he smiled in triumph. "Let's see. I have two houses on this property. That looks like five hundred dollars you owe me."

I thumbed through my available cash. "No way. You can't charge me that much."

Frank held out the card listing the rent charges. "Look here."

"I don't have it. Let me pay you a hundred, and let's go on."

"No, but I'll take your Illinois, Indiana, and Kentucky as payment."

I tossed cards haphazardly into the box. "Nope. I'm done playing." And I tipped the game board with my toe, scattering pieces. Then I stood up and walked away, leaving Frank with the mess.

Benny cried for no reason at all and Pete and Ralph argued loudly over who was the best baseball player, Ted Williams or Jackie Robinson.

"That's it," Mr. Garrett roared. "No radio. No games. In your beds right now. Ten minutes until lights out."

There was a rumble of muted protests, but our bare feet padded reluctantly toward the bathroom or beds. I didn't go to the bathroom because I needed to get Lee up later.

"Mr. Garrett has a date with his bottle," Bobby whispered as we climbed into our beds.

I nodded. "He isn't happy about the tournament. He keeps looking for ways to give us detentions. We need to stick together. I shouldn't have argued with Frank about the Monopoly game."

Bobby cocked his head and waited.

"I know," I sighed. "I need to tell Frank I'm sorry and tell God I'm sorry."

"Lights out!" Mr. Garrett's voice boomed across the bedroom. John and Lee's bare feet slapped the wooden floor as they hurried to their beds. I could picture the scowl on Mr. Garrett's face as he watched them. A few seconds later, and darkness blanketed the room.

The boys collectively held their breaths for one minute, two, and then the whispering began.

"Frank," I called to my friend on the other side of the room. "Frank, I'm sorry about Monopoly."

"That's okay, Matthew. Everybody has a bad day now and then."

I waited a while longer before slipping out of my bed and getting on my knees. I wanted to keep things right between me and God. I bowed my head. At that moment the room flooded with light.

"Matthew Freeman, are you out of your bed?" Mr. Garrett's voice thundered over our beds.

I bolted to my feet. "No, sir. I mean, yes, sir, I was, but I was just praying—"

Almost gleefully, it seemed to me, Mr. Garrett interrupted. "Doesn't matter why you were out of bed. It's lights out and you're to be in bed. Guess that means a detention for you. I'll write it up and give it to Miss Bailey tomorrow."

"You can strap me if you want." I was okay with anything but a detention that would make me ineligible for the tournament. And incapable of earning the money for Betsy's braces.

He moved to stand beside my bed, his features twisted in a smirking smile. He leaned down in my face, and I smelled the alcohol on his breath. "No, I'm not strapping you. I'll let Miss Bailey handle it her way. Now"— his voice growled, and the smirk disappeared—"get in that bed and don't get out again."

I finished my prayer, desperately wishing I'd remained in bed. Now, besides asking for forgiveness for the argument with Frank, I pleaded to somehow escape detention and remain in the marble tournament.

Chapter 16

The numbers floated around my head like gnats on a summer evening. Thanks to the diligent work of both Miss Jones and Sharon, I could do long division. But not this morning. I nibbled on the eraser end of my pencil. Maybe Miss Jones would let me use the restroom. We were supposed to use it during restroom breaks, not class time, but she occasionally made an exception.

Just as I was about to raise my hand, I heard the tap, tap, tap of shoes up the main stairs. I kept my face toward my desk, but my eyes followed Miss Jones as she moved to the rear of the classroom and stood in quiet conversation with Miss Bailey. Then came the softer sound of Miss Jones's shoes as she approached my desk.

"Matthew, Miss Bailey would like a word with you in the hall."

"Sure." I dropped my pencil on the empty paper and hurried out.

Miss Bailey looked tall and stern in her dark skirt and white shirt. She held a paper in one hand which she kind of waved at me. "Hello, Matthew. Before he left this morning, Mr. Garrett handed me this report. I'm sorry, but I'm going to have to place you on detention. Do you know what this means?"

I squeezed my eyes shut tightly in an attempt to keep tears from escaping. Without raising my head, I nodded and mumbled, "Yes, ma'am."

"Matthew, look up at me."

I looked up and a lone tear found its way out and trickled down my cheek.

"I wish I didn't have to do this. I know you wanted to go to that marble tournament and you had very noble reasons for wanting to win. But I can't go against one of our staff members. Until further notice, you are on detention. No outdoor time, no off-campus trips, bed at seven. Do you understand?"

I sniffed a little, determined not to let any more tears fall. "Yes, ma'am."

"Now go on back to class and don't be disrespectful to Mr. Garrett again. We're lucky to have a young man like him to supervise our boys at night."

Disrespectful? I wondered just what Mr. Garrett had written on the form.

It was my night to get up and take Lee, so I downed another glass of water before crawling into my bed. The other boys were laughing at something on the radio. I'd never felt so alone, and I longed for the touch of my mom's hand and the sound of Gabby's giggle. I wasn't an orphan; I had a mom who loved me.

I reached under my bed for my bag of marbles and shifted the round, hard shapes in my hands. Even when I'd thought I was doing some good, my plans had gone all wrong.

Dropping them back into my box, I buried my head in my pillow and sobbed out my prayers.

Much later, my full bladder woke me up. I went first, then woke Lee. Afterward, I followed him back to his bed, pulling the rough, gray blanket back up around his skinny shoulders.

I was heading back to my bed when I heard the whimper. It sounded like a hurt puppy. Was someone having a bad dream? I paused in between the two rows of beds, trying to determine where it was coming from. Squinting through the darkness, I could make out a small shape, huddled on the bed opposite Lee's.

I tiptoed over. "What's wrong, Benny?"

He sniffled once and leaned against me. "My froat hurts."

I patted his head. It felt very hot, and his blond curls were damp. An icy chill of fear shot through me. I knew polio was contagious. What if Benny had polio, too?

"I'll go get Mr. Garrett for you, Benny. Here, get under your blankets again. I'll get him and be right back."

He sniffed again but lay back on the pillow. I hurried down the row until I got to Bobby's bed. There would be safety in numbers. "Bobby! Bobby! Wake up."

"Not my turn to take Lee. I don't have to go." He rolled over and pulled his blanket over his head.

I jerked the blanket out of his grasp and onto the floor. "It's not Lee. It's Benny. He's sick."

Bobby sat up, blinking and running a hand through hair that stuck out in every direction. "Benny? Sick?"

"He's real sick, like needing-a-doctor sick. I think we need to get Mr. Garrett."

"Ohhhh." He yawned. Bobby was sure hard to wake up. But I think he started to understand. He stood up. "Let's go."

We padded out the door in our bare feet and went down the hall. At the landing we stopped. We knew Mr. Garrett's room was down the hall, before the girls' wing, but we'd never gone there before. I swallowed hard and took a few more steps. When we got to his room, the heavy wooden door was closed.

Bobby nudged me. "Knock."

I knocked softly. "Mr. Garrett?" After a few minutes, I tried knocking again, harder. Finally, both Bobby and I pounded on the door and shouted, "Mr. Garrett!" There was still no answer.

I reached out and grabbed the heavy metal doorknob. I hesitated a moment, then turned it. It rotated, and the door swung in. Mr. Garrett lay stretched out on his bed, fully dressed, with a bottle resting against his chest.

"What's going on, boys?" Mrs. McKale, the girls' supervisor, stood in the hall. Her bathrobe's belt, knotted at her middle, made her look like a plump pillow tied with a ribbon.

"Benny is real sick, and we can't get Mr. Garrett to wake up." I trembled a little, waiting for her response. We were out of our beds and almost to the girls' wing. Who would believe we just wanted to help Benny?

108

Her slippers made a slap-thump sound in the wide hallway as she crossed and stood between Bobby and me. When she peered into Mr. Garrett's room, I heard a sharp gasp. Then, with a firm hand on each of our shoulders, she turned and guided us back down the hallway.

"I'll see to Benny, boys. Mr. Garrett doesn't seem to be in a position to do that now."

We led Mrs. McKale to Benny's bed. After checking him over, she wrapped him in his blanket, picked him up, and held him like a much younger child. "Thanks for letting us know about Benny, boys. I'm taking him to my room so I can give him some aspirin and keep an eye on him. You two go back to bed now."

As I lay down, I remembered to pray, "God help Benny to get better. Please, let it not be polio."

"Boys! Time to get up!" A voice that was not Mr. Garrett's called from the doorway. In the bed next to me, Bobby groaned and rolled over.

I tugged his blanket off. "Bobby, Miss Bailey is calling us."

The name must have registered because he tumbled out of bed, onto the floor and squinted up at me. "Where's Mr. Garrett?"

"Don't know, but I'm definitely getting up on time." I pulled my pajamas off and reached for my clean clothes in one motion.

Later, in answer to our questions, Miss Bailey told us, "Mr. Garrett is gone. I will be supervising the older boys until a replacement is found."

If not for Miss Bailey's presence, we would have broken out into shouts and cheers, and as we marched down the stairs for our breakfast duties, there was an air of celebration. It felt like Christmas and the Fourth

109

of July all wrapped up in one. We shared the story with Jemma as we dished up bowls of oatmeal.

She listened intently, but her hands kept busy serving. "Well then," she said as I paused to get another stack of bowls, "what happened to Benny?"

Suddenly, we ceased our chatter. Not one of us had thought of Benny this morning. Just then, we heard the noise of the girls as they lined up for breakfast. At the end of the line, Mrs. McKale bustled in. Bobby and I dropped what we were doing and hurried out of the kitchen.

Bobby was the first to reach her. "How's Benny?"

"Why, what good friends that little boy has!" She smiled down at us. "I think he'll be fine in a day or two. He's in the infirmary with Nurse Cadie today, but he thinks he wants to try a bowl of oatmeal, so I'm going to take him a tray."

"He doesn't have polio?" I whispered.

Her face sobered. "The doctor will check him over, of course, but no, it doesn't look like polio. Just a cold with a sore throat."

I let out the breath I'd been holding, then realized we'd left Jemma to do everything in the kitchen by herself. "Thanks!" I shouted at Mrs. McKale as I weaved back between the tables to the kitchen, where I handed out steaming bowls of oatmeal with a smile. Last in line was Betsy in her wheelchair. One of the older girls, whose name I couldn't remember, pushed her.

"Hi, Matthew." She reached for the tray the other girl had filled. "How's the marble playing?"

110

"Okay," I mumbled.

"I think it's exciting that Pete and Ralph and the others are going to play in that tournament. But I wish you were going, too. I understand they have to take the oldest boys, but you're the best marble player. Do you still have your champion blue shooter? Wouldn't it be neat if someone from the Children's Home actually won the National Marble Tournament? I wonder what they would do with the prize money."

The girl pushing her chair moved toward the tables, but Betsy turned her head and kept talking. I nodded and tried to muster a smile at her, but inside I felt terrible. She had no idea that I wanted to win so I could buy her braces, but now there was no way I could do that.

Since it was Saturday, we had our usual routine of chores. We cleaned our room, swept the floor, and dusted in the game room. Then we washed down the sinks and toilets in the bathroom. In the afternoon, Mrs. McKale supervised the boys who had no visitors. Delilah, the woman who did our laundry, supervised the girls, since Miss Bailey needed to greet people. The boys who were going to the tournament practiced without the usual bickering. With Nationals only a week away, there was no time to waste. Bobby and I watched the games and filled in when someone was called away.

"Ralph. Ralph Bloyer." Miss Bailey stood at the door of the game room.

"What'd I do now?" Ralph grumbled quietly as he scooped up his marbles. Then he looked at Bobby and me. "I want my place back; she can't gripe at me too long on visiting day."

Ralph followed Miss Bailey down the hall, and it was a long time before he returned. When he did, his face was shining with a huge ear-to-ear grin. "I'm gettin' outta here!"

Within a few seconds, every boy in the place was gathered around. Even Lee dropped the top he was playing with and followed John across the room.

"I'm gonna work on a farm," Ralph said. "Guy named Ralph, same as me, came in and needs help this summer. So they chose me, 'cause I'm the biggest guy here and pretty strong."

Frank's eyes were envious. "So you got a mom and dad?"

Ralph's grin faded a little. "Not exactly. I'll be working and getting paid. And if they don't need me next fall, I'll jus' move on and get myself another job." He looked around the room. "Not comin' back here, that's for sure."

Donovan asked the question I'd been thinking. "When do you leave?"

"Tuesday. Miss Jones will give me my exams on Monday. So's I can pass eighth grade. Then Tuesday morning…off to my farm. I'm gonna go pack now."

He moved toward our bedroom, with several boys trailing after him and pelting him with questions.

I sat wondering. If Ralph and I weren't going to be in the marble tournament, would Miss Bailey choose two other boys to take our spots?

Chapter 17

My last forkful of biscuits and gravy hung between my plate and my mouth. Miss Bailey had just asked the boys to remain in the dining room for a meeting after breakfast. It could only mean one thing. We had a new boys' supervisor.

An older man, round as my grandpa and looking about the same age, stood behind her. Little, wire-rimmed glasses perched on a bulbous nose, and bright-blue eyes peered out through the lenses. His flannel shirt stretched rather tightly across his middle, but it was tucked neatly into his pants.

I shoved the rest of my breakfast in my mouth, washed it down with juice, and hurried to the kitchen. "Jemma, we're getting a new supervisor."

"I see, Matthew. Here, take this pan to the sink. We'll let it soak a bit. He's an answer to prayer, now isn't he?"

"Yeah. I hope he doesn't carry a strap."

He wasn't carrying one when Miss Bailey introduced him. "Boys, this is Mr. Benson. He is our new supervisor, and he will be here tonight after school. I expect all of you"—her stern gaze seemed to take in each one of us—"to show him respect and to help him as he adjusts to his new job. Now say hello."

We chorused our hellos, jostling each other a little, suddenly shy and embarrassed.

"I'm sure we'll get along just fine, won't we, boys?" Mr. Benson had a cheerful smile that made his eyes twinkle behind the glasses.

"Line up now." Miss Bailey motioned to us, and we quickly grouped ourselves single file. She looked behind her at Mr. Benson. "Why don't you follow us while I walk the boys to the classroom? Then you can complete your paper work in my office."

The school day seemed to last forever. In the afternoon, we had a party, because it was Ralph's last day with us. Jemma made chocolate cupcakes with thick fudge frosting, and we washed them down with an extra bottle of milk. Ralph picked a word and we played hangman on the chalkboard. The closer the clock crept to four, the more fidgety we became, twisting in our seats to see whether Mr. Benson had come. At precisely 3:55, he stood at the door, and we hurried to line up. No one shoved or pushed; we used our best manners to impress the new supervisor.

"I understand you generally have outdoor time now," Mr. Benson said.

Frank, who had gotten the coveted first-in-line position, nodded. "That's right. We go outside unless it's raining."

"Follow me." He led the way, and we thumped down the stairs and out to a sun-drenched spring afternoon. We spilled out the door and over the playground. Pete, Frank, and Donovan drew the circle and lag line. Bobby and I leaned against the playground fence, watching.

114

"You two playing?" Donovan asked.

"Sure." I dug out my blue shooter. Frank won the toss and knuckled down. A shadow dropped over the circle, and the five of us froze in position, slowly raising our heads to look up at Mr. Benson.

"Play away, boys. I just came to watch."

We'd never had an adult show any interest before, but after a few minutes, we almost forgot he was there; we were focused on the game. When I scooped up the last marble to win, he stepped forward and patted my back.

"Not bad, young man. Let me see that shooter." Mr. Benson held up the blue marble to the sunlight, squinting and rolling it between his finger and thumb. Then he handed it back to me. "Are you going to be in the marble tournament on Saturday?"

I hung my head. "No, sir. I can't go."

"Can't go? Why ever not?"

"I had a detention."

"And what was the reason for this detention?"

"I got out of bed after lights out."

"What were you doing?"

I scuffed my shoe through the dirt. "Praying."

"Hmmm." Mr. Benson looked at Bobby. "Are you going?"

Bobby shook the forelock of red hair out of his eyes. "No. They chose the oldest boys first."

"Hmmm," he said again. Shortly after that, he left the marble game and stood by the swings, pushing Benny who'd recovered from his sore throat.

After supper and chores, Mr. Benson played cards with us in the game room. And by the time he called lights out and we crawled into our beds, I think every one of us remembered to pray, "Thank You, God, for sending Mr. Benson."

The next afternoon, Miss Bailey was at our classroom at 3:55. When I saw her, my stomach flip-flopped. Where was Mr. Benson? Had we lost him already? What if Mr. Garrett came back?

"Boys and girls, I know you are all aware that a few of our boys are going to the National Marble Tournament this Saturday."

The classroom grew so quiet, I was sure everyone could hear the thumping of my heart.

"Due to some recent developments, there are some changes."

I held my breath, and was sure every boy in the classroom did the same.

"The boys who will represent Taylor Springs Children's Home in the National Marble Tournament are: Pete, Frank, Donovan, Bobby, and Matthew."

The entire classroom, boys and girls, erupted in cheers and shouting.

Miss Bailey held up her hands. "Boys and girls there is no need for this much noise. I have one more announcement. Because Mr. Benson has offered to chaperone, any boy or girl who would like to attend and watch is welcome to do so. I am sending a sign-up list around now. Please put your name on the list if you want to be included. This privilege can be revoked, of course, if there is any misbehavior between now and Saturday."

The cheers of the entire classroom drowned out her last words. This time she didn't scold us. As a matter of fact, as she left with her list, I thought I saw her smile.

Chapter 18

Somehow, Mr. Benson managed to borrow a school bus from the Taylor Springs High School. We piled onto the bus, the five marble players commandeering the front two seats and everyone else tumbling in after them.

"What about Betsy?" I asked as I scooted next to Bobby, making room on the seat for Donovan.

"I don't see how they would get her wheelchair in here." Bobby peered out the window. "There she is with Miss Bailey, waving to us."

It didn't seem fair to leave her behind, but Bobby was right. There was no way her wheel chair would fit through the doors.

It was a short ride to the county fairgrounds, where the tournament would be held. We jumped out of the bus and looked around in amazement. Hundreds of boys were rushing back and forth, many of them followed by an older person, probably a mom or dad. A large sign with a black arrow pointed the way to the registration table.

"Let's go register." Pete led, and the other four players followed.

At the registration table, a young woman with blond hair pulled back in a ponytail took our names and checked us off on a list. "So, you're the boys from the Children's Home, huh? It's so nice they let you out so you could play in the tournament. Just like regular kids."

I wasn't sure how to reply, so I just gave her a quick smile and took the number she gave me.

"Pin your numbers on your sleeve. The first games start at nine a.m. in the exhibition hall." She pointed in the direction of a long gray building. Then, checking a small silver wrist watch, she added, "You have forty minutes."

"Just like regular kids," Frank mimicked. "She makes it sound like we're lepers or something." He scowled at her as we walked away.

"Awww, that's just how some folks talk. Don't pay any attention to that. We're gonna show them we're champ-ee-ons." Donovan clasped his hands over his head and shook them.

That made us all laugh. Bobby helped me pin my number on my sleeve, and then I helped him. I wore number forty-six and he was forty-seven.

I twisted and turned to see everything as we followed Pete toward the exhibition hall. Boys crowded and jostled us on every side. Everyone seemed to be headed in the same direction.

The carnival-like smells, popcorn, people, and even faint animal smells from the original competitors at the fairgrounds washed over me. My stomach felt like it was doing gymnastics. At breakfast, I'd barely managed two bites of Jemma's pancakes. When I'd returned my plate to the kitchen, she'd smothered me against her floury apron. "You do us proud, you hear? Why don't you take these for a snack?" She tucked a package of oatmeal raisin cookies into my pocket. Now, I could hear the wax paper crinkling when I walked.

As we entered the exhibition hall, the buzz of hundreds of excited, nervous boys hit us. Pete stopped, and we bumped into each other like a line of dominoes. Bleacher-type seating lined the oval arena. The playing area was fenced off with white boards. Ten individual rings, each with a border of wood, a painted circle, and a lag line, covered the floor. Men in red vests gestured wildly, directing the milling crowd.

"Competitors only on the floor." When the nearest red-vested man saw our numbered sleeves, he pointed to a huge chart pinned on the wall. "You can check there for your first game, boys. Then have the official check your shooters."

We weaved our way through the mass of boys until we reached the chart. It took a minute to understand what it was. The chart would display the ring, players, and winners for each round. A game consisted of seven innings; the player with the most points would win. Then the matches would be made for the next round. We found our numbers listed. I was scheduled to play in Ring 6, Bobby in Ring 7. Since there were only ten rings, we had to wait for the fourth game. Officials at each ring were checking in players and inspecting their shooters.

I reached into my right pants pocket for my trusty Old Blue. My fingers scraped the bottom of the pocket and found no marble. I quickly switched, pulled out the package of cookies, and dug deep into my left pocket. Again, I felt only the seam at the bottom. Panicking, I jammed both hands down and scrabbled frantically. Then I carefully tugged the pockets inside out. My winning shooter, my taw, was gone.

"Where's your blue marble?" Bobby's face wrinkled with concern.

"I always put it in here." I patted my right pocket, which hung against my pant leg like a deflated balloon.

"A back pocket? A shirt pocket?"

My hands patted my front and backside, knowing what they would find. Nothing. "I can't play," I whispered, "not without Old Blue."

Bobby pulled out his shooter, a large yellow-orange orb. "Listen, Matthew, you're the better player. You can use mine."

I shook my head. "No, I won't take yours. Besides, I can't win any games without my shooter."

Bobby's blue eyes looked at me with an expression as stern as Miss Jones's when someone had misbehaved. "Some trust in chariots ... and some trust in blue marbles ... but we will remember the name of the Lord our God..."

"They are brought down and fallen; but we are risen, and stand upright." I finished the verses with him.

"You can do this. It wasn't the blue marble that gave you marble-playing talent. It was God. And whether you win or whether you lose, you play for Him." Bobby held out his shooter.

I hesitated. Just then I heard someone call my name from the crowds jamming the stands. I twisted around, looking. Bobby saw them first. Jemma pushed Betsy in her chair, and they both shouted and waved. We waved back, and I wondered whether Jemma had walked all the way from the Children's Home.

"Okay, I'll do it." I curled my hand into a fist around the marble Bobby had dropped into my palm. "Because Betsy still needs those braces. But, come on; let's ask if we can share it." I pulled his hand toward Ring 6.

The official at the ring held Bobby's marble and considered our request. "Well, I guess there's nothing in the rules to prevent you from sharing. The only hitch would be if you both needed the shooter at the same time."

"Then he gets it." Bobby jerked his thumb in my direction.

Suddenly weak-kneed with nervousness, I sat down on the bench facing the rings. Bobby sat beside me. His head was down, and I knew he was praying for us.

Chapter 19

I eyed the boy who stepped into Ring 6 with me. He stood a head taller and looked at least fourteen, with adolescent pimples showing on his forehead. He nodded hello, but his eyebrows were drawn together, either frowning at me or concentrating on the game. The ring official set up the thirteen target marbles with a template, each an exact distance from the others.

He directed us to move to the edge of the chalk circle with one foot back against the wooden ring. Then when his whistle tweeted, we tossed our shooters across the ring toward the lag line. Bobby's yellow-orange marble rolled gently across the lag line and came to a stop in the dirt, less than a quarter inch away. My opponent's marble halted an inch before the line. I would shoot first.

I stood and brushed off my knees. With a glance toward the stands, where Jemma and Betsy sat with Mr. Benson, I knelt. Just as I did every night beside my bed at the Children's Home. Kneeling to pray, kneeling to play. Today there didn't seem to be a difference. The crowd, the official, the kneeling players in the other rings seemed to fade away as I focused on the thirteen target marbles set in a cross formation.

I carefully took aim at the center of the cross. My shooter hit the center marble with a solid thunk, and it rolled out of the circle. I scored my first point. I moved around the ring to get into position for my next shot. Flick! Click! Flick! Click! The marbles flew across the circle. When a marble rolled out, I could hear Bobby's voice, "Swell job! Neato!" His voice sounded far away.

Flick! Click! A green marble rolled out. "That's a stick!" the official called as he stepped into the ring. I had hit seven marbles out and won the first game.

I quickly passed the shooter to Bobby. Although he won the lag toss, a stocky boy in a felt hat defeated him. He handed the marble back to me, and we went to check the charts to see in which ring my next game would be, and whether the other boys from the Children's Home had advanced. Pete had won his first game, but both Donovan and Frank had lost. I moved to Ring 3 for my second game.

Two games later, I had three wins and had earned a spot in the semifinals. A man with a large megaphone announced play would resume in two hours. I looked around for my companions.

"Matthew! Over here!" Mr. Benson waved to Bobby and me. Pete, Donovan, and Frank were with him and all the older kids who'd come to watch, but I didn't see Jemma and Betsy. As we wove our way through the crowd, he explained, "Mrs. Foster made us a picnic lunch. We're to meet her at the south end of the parade grounds by the big oak tree."

I started to ask Pete whether he'd won his second game, but the pouty look on his face made it clear. I decided not to talk about my games either.

When we got to the parade grounds, I was glad Jemma had told us exactly where to meet her. The grassy area held hundreds of people gathering in little bunches, with picnic baskets and tablecloths spread out over the grass.

"Why don't we go to McDonald's for lunch?" I joked.

"What's McDonald's?" Donovan asked as he helped Mr. Benson spread out a big quilt.

"Just someplace I used to go to eat with my mom and sister." I sighed, but too much was happening for me to feel unhappy.

After everyone found a place to sit on the quilt, we bowed our heads and chanted, "God is great. God is good. And we thank Him, for our food."

But in my heart, I was thankful for so much more than the food.

Betsy handed me a sandwich wrapped neatly in waxed paper. "So, how did you get here?" I asked.

"Jemma's husband brought us in their wagon." Betsy pointed across the grass to where two horses were tied. "He stayed with the horses because they get nervous around all the cars."

"You played really well this morning." Betsy said to me as she handed sandwiches to Pete, Frank, Donovan, and Bobby.

"The important games are still to come." I unwrapped the thick roast beef sandwich and wondered if I could eat it. My stomach was still doing flips. I didn't want to get in the marble ring and throw up.

"You'll do fine." She twisted in her chair, straining to reach the picnic basket with the empty sandwich container. Oh, how I wished she could walk again!

After lunch, the other boys, Mr. Benson, and I walked back to the exhibition hall, while Jemma and Betsy took the picnic basket and the quilt back to the wagon.

Only competitors for the final games were allowed in the rings, so I walked to Ring 3 alone. Each of the remaining eight contestants would play at least three games. And someone would be the champion and take home one hundred dollars. I took a deep breath and pulled out Bobby's shooter for the official to inspect.

Chapter 20

My marble rolled just past the lag line, less than an inch. But my opponent, a short, black-haired boy with glasses, lobbed his shooter, and it rolled right to the line and stopped. He would play first. He knelt and knuckled down. He shot fluidly, almost as if he didn't take aim, but his shots were accurate. Flick! Click! Flick! Click! He had two marbles out in rapid succession.

He moved around the ring. He reminded me of a cat, crouching before he pounced. Flick! Click! Another marble rolled out. Was I even going to get a chance to play, or would he get a stick?

Flick! Click! Flick! Click! Two more. He moved again, knelt, and knuckled down. Flick! Click! Without standing up, he scooted to the right and took aim. Flick! Click! If this marble went out, he had won the game, and I'd lost any chance at the championship. The target rolled to the circle and stopped.

Was it in or out? The referee would make the decision. The noise of the crowd hushed as he stepped around the ring and peered down at the marble. Then he knelt and looked at it from the right, from the left, and from above. I held my breath.

"The marble remains in!" he announced, flourishing his arm toward me.

It was my turn. I would have to shoot out all seven remaining marbles to win this game. Glancing up at the stands, my eyes searched the crowd for Betsy and Jemma. They weren't there. Had they left? I turned and walked around the ring, plotting my strategy. As I hit out one marble, I wanted to be in a good position to get the next one.

Suddenly, above the noise of the crowd, I heard a voice. "The blue marble! The blue marble!" My first thought was that my shooter had been found. Then I saw her. Jemma had pushed Betsy's chair around, and she was frantically waving at me and shouting, "The blue marble."

I looked again at the arrangement of marbles left in the circle. The blue-swirled marble was in the center. If I knocked it out...and then the green one...and then...I knelt and knuckled down, taking aim at the blue marble. Flick! Click! It was out. I hit the green one, then an orange, a black, a white, and two yellow ones.

Then I took aim at the last marble, a green cat's eye. Flick! Click! It rolled out. I'd won the first round of the championships.

It would be a few minutes before my next game, so I moved back and waved a thank you to Betsy. Then I waited for my name to be called. My next game would be against Steven McConnell, a slender boy who played marbles as if his life depended on it. I'd watched him play earlier and knew he was good.

I heard my name called for Ring 3. Steven and I lined up. I won the lag toss, so I hoped for a stick. I knuckled down and took aim. One, two, three, four marbles in a row were mine. The fifth target marble was near the circle's edge. Click! Bobby's orange shooter hit it solidly. The marble shot outside the circle, but the shooter kept rolling. *Stop! Stop!* Then, like a disobedient toddler, it rolled slowly out of the circle. I earned five points, but the inning was over, and it was Steven's turn. Unless he made an error, I would lose the game.

Steven went to his knees, his face hardened into fierce concentration. He aimed carefully and hit out his target. Then shaking the kinks out of his arms, he stepped around the ring. Two more marbles went out. He scooted to where his shooter had stopped and took aim again. The target marble spun out, then another. He aimed at a marble across the circle. He would need to have some speed. Flick! Clunk! The target marble split into two pieces. One piece flew out of the circle, and the other wobbled a few inches and stopped.

The referee's whistle tweeted and we froze. He stepped into the circle to inspect the broken marble. He picked up the pieces one by one, twisting them in his fingers and holding them up to each other.

Finally he spoke, looking at the announcer with the megaphone, so he could repeat what was said for the audience. "The target marble broke. The larger piece remained in the circle. No point for the shooter. The game will continue with the other player."

That was me. I was the other player. I dropped to my knees so quickly that I skinned one of them on the border of the ring. *Steady does it*, I imagined Betsy telling me. I took a breath and let it out slowly. Then I took aim at my first target, an orange-swirled marble in the center. Flick! Click! It was out. The last marble was another blue one. I aimed carefully.

Flick! Click! The marble spun out of the circle. I won again! One more game, and I would win the National Marble Tournament.

There were three games left. The first would be played to determine the fifth and sixth place winners, then a game for third and fourth place winners, and then the championship game for first and second place. I watched as the two boys played in the center ring. Leaning against the rail in the stands was a mom-looking woman with long brown hair and a pinkish print dress. She called, "Do your best, Barney!"

Suddenly, I wanted to be home more than anything else in the world. I wanted my mom cheering me on. I wanted Gabby holding onto me and begging me to play Barbies. I wanted the warmth and love of my family. If I could have gone home by just walking out of the exhibition hall and into 2016, I would have done it.

But I looked around, and it was still 1946. And I was being called to play the championship game of the National Marble Tournament.

The announcer's megaphone boomed. "What a day this has been at the National Marble Tournament in Taylor Springs, Missouri. We have been privileged to watch so many talented young players. And now, the best of the best. At the center marble ring we have your championship tournament with Larry Joe Stillman of Princeville, Iowa, and our own Matthew Freeman from Taylor Springs, Missouri. For those of you who don't know, Matthew is an orphan from the Taylor Springs Children's Home." He smiled at me like I was special for losing my family.

I lifted my head. I could see them all lined up: Pete, Donovan, Frank, Bobby, Mr. Benson, Jemma, and Betsy. They all waved at me. I gave a little wave, then shook out my arms. I had a game to win.

I won the lag toss. Larry Joe stepped out of the way and I knelt at the circle's edge and focused on the cross of marbles. Flick! Click! And the first target marble was out. Flick! Click! Flick! Click! Two and three.

I hit a rhythm: step around, kneel, flick the shooter. Four, five and six shot out. I aimed at a blue marble, almost the same sky blue as my missing shooter. Bobby's orange marble sailed out of my hand, hit the blue marble and off it went. Go! Go! It rolled to the edge and stopped directly on the circle.

I held my breath as the referee stepped over to make the decision on the marble. "Marble is in!" he shouted. Then, nodding at Larry Joe, he motioned me back.

No! You're wrong, I wanted to shout. It can't be in. I have to win for Betsy.

Larry Joe dropped to one knee and aimed. Then he moved slightly to the right and aimed again. Then he backed up and aimed again. Then his black shooter shot across the circle, hitting a white marble and knocking it out. An orange marble and a green one quickly followed. Each time he aimed, it seemed like he had to first move right, then left.

A red marble rolled out, then another green one. Two marbles were left, a white one and the blue one sitting on the circle. Larry Joe aimed, then scooted right, aimed, then scooted left. Then his shooter flew toward the blue marble. Click! A solid hit, and the marble rolled out.

His shooter wobbled along the circle's edge and came to a stop. Larry Joe stood up and moved toward it. The referee's whistle tweeted, and Larry stopped.

"It's in!" Larry Joe's voice was high and trembly.

The referee didn't speak as he knelt to examine the position of the black shooter. "Out!" came the decision.

I still had a chance. All I had to do was knock the white marble out of the circle and I would win. I knelt for the last time. Flick! I sent the orange shooter on its way. Click! The white marble spun slowly out of the circle. Above the roar of the crowd, I thought I heard Betsy's voice. "You did it, Matthew. I knew you could."

Within a few minutes, we were all on the winners' stand. Starting with the sixth-place winner, the announcer shouted out the player's name and presented a ribbon. When he said, "First place, Matthew Freeman," I thought I would burst. He handed me an envelope, shook my hand, and laughed. "Bet you're going to get all the toys you never had."

"Thank you, sir." I remembered my manners just as I left the ring. Mr. Benson, the boys, Jemma, and Betsy circled around me as I stepped off the exhibition hall floor.

Pete slapped me on the back. "You did us proud!"

Donovan grinned. "Pretty good for an *orphan boy.*"

"An orphan who knows in whom to trust," I added and the others nodded. I whispered a quick thank-you prayer.

Then I peeked inside the envelope at the crisp bills. One hundred dollars would be a lot of money, even in 2016.

Smiling, I dropped the envelope in Betsy's lap. "This is for you. Now you can get those braces so you can walk again."

Her eyes widened, and her mouth opened as if she were going to say something, but nothing came out. Finally she said, "Oh, no, Matthew. I can't take your prize money."

"I want to give it to you." I looked at Jemma, my eyes pleading for her help.

"He wants you to have it, honey. Just say thanks." Jemma patted Betsy gently on the arm.

Betsy glanced over her shoulder at Jemma, then back at me. Her brown eyes sparkled. "Matthew, I don't know what to say."

"Say thank you to the National Marble Champ-ee-on!" I chirruped spinning around and taking hold of Betsy's chair. "I'll push you to the wagon."

I trotted behind the chair, out of the exhibition hall, and toward the parking lot. I could see Jemma's husband's wagon with the horses hitched to it. I rolled the chair through the dirt, my feet dancing behind it. Betsy used one hand to hold on to the chair; the other clutched the prize money. Bobby, Frank, Donovan, and Pete ran beside us. Jemma, Mr. Benson, and the rest of the kids trailed behind.

Suddenly I jerked the chair to a halt, almost spilling Betsy in the dirt. Directly in front of us, shining like a tiny piece of the sky, all rolled up in a glass ball, was my blue marble. I let go of the wheel chair, dropped to my knees, and scooped it up out of the dirt.

And then I was spinning, whirling, dust rising around me. I felt like a rag doll tossed in the air. When the spinning stopped, I opened my eyes. I sat in the dirt. Canterbury Lane lay in front of me. I saw the parked bulldozer, and across the street was my house. It was 2016, and I was home again.

Dusty stood a few feet away with his skateboard under his arm. "Decided to come skating? Great. Let's go."

Slowly, I stood, brushing dust off my pants. "No." I shook my head firmly. "Mom needs me at home."

"Mom! Gabby!" I took off running home to my family.

Gabby met me at the back door. "Mom says you have to watch me."

I reached out and gave her a huge hug. "I can't think of anything I'd rather do. Shall we play Barbies?"

Her brown eyes got big, and then she hopped up and down like a striped frog, and hollered, "Yes! I do."

Mom called from the office, "Matthew, where have you been?"

"Oh, just around the neighborhood." I smiled. They'd never believe where a blue marble could take you.

Questions for Discussion

1. Have you ever wished your family would disappear?

2. What things are different in your life compared to 1946?

3. Which of the children from the orphanage would you pick for a friend and why?

4. What did Betsy and Bobby do that showed their character?

5. Why do you think Matthew could play marbles so well?

6. How is playing marbles like playing your favorite game? How is it different?

7. How did Matthew's feelings about his mom and Gabby change?

8. How did Matthew's view of trusting God change? What events brought that about?

To my readers:

I pray that *The Blue Marble* has not only been fun to read, but that it has blessed and encouraged you to trust God for all things, little and big.

Your purchase of this book has blessed others, too. All author's proceeds go to Pour International to maintain a home for abandoned and orphaned babies and children in Swaziland, Africa. For more information on this organization you may contact ScottBorg@yahoo.com or www.info@pourinternational.org

For I will pour water on the thirsty land,
and streams on the dry ground;
I will pour out my Spirit on your offspring
and my blessing on your descendants.
(Isaiah 44:3)

32345112R00080

Made in the USA
San Bernardino, CA
03 April 2016